THE Day the Cat Ran Away

Nancy Gotter Gates

W❂RLDWIDE®

TORONTO • NEW YORK • LONDON
AMSTERDAM • PARIS • SYDNEY • HAMBURG
STOCKHOLM • ATHENS • TOKYO • MILAN
MADRID • WARSAW • BUDAPEST • AUCKLAND

Recycling programs
for this product may
not exist in your area.

The Day the Cat Ran Away

A Worldwide Mystery/January 2015

First published by Cottage Place Publishing

ISBN-13: 978-0-373-26927-3

Copyright © 2013 by Nancy Gotter Gates

Printed in U.S.A.

Acknowledgments

Thanks as always to my wonderful writing group for their insightful comments on my manuscript: Harol Marshall, Lynette Hall Hampton and Betty DiMeo.

ONE

"So, Vi-OH-LA, what's on your agenda for this afternoon?"

"Absolutely nothing, Ty-RONE," I said. If he thought he was going to annoy me by calling me by my full name I could play that game as well. I guess that proved we were bored. If only I'd known what the day had in store for me.

My best friend Ty and I were savoring our Sunday brunch at Glendon Hills Retirement Center in Guilford City, North Carolina. (We usually refer to it as GH and sometimes *Geezer Heaven*.) It was mid-July and hot as Hades, though as usual I had on a light sweater for the dining room is always cooler than I like. Ty, on the other hand, thought it was too warm and had taken off his tie, which he wore only on Sunday, and unbuttoned the top button of his shirt. Typical for each of us.

Sunday is the one day we don't have table service. The only meal is a buffet-style brunch and the food choices are plentiful. I had waffles piled high with strawberries and whipped cream along with a Western omelet. Ty chose roast beef, asparagus and salad. That's why I outweigh him by probably twenty pounds. Of course I am big-boned and two inches taller, and he is thin and wiry. His head full of steel gray curls almost makes up the difference in spite of the fact he tries without success to keep it slicked down.

"Dessert?" I asked after we'd cleaned our plates.

He cocked an eyebrow. "Wasn't that what the waffles and strawberries were?"

I gave him a look of mock horror. "Of course not! That

was breakfast and the omelet was my lunch. Now I want some of that rice pudding."

Along with the usual cakes and pies, on Sunday we always have a huge chafing dish of either rice or bread pudding. I think it's a nod to the underlying omnipresence of nostalgia that permeates GH, calling up gustatory memories of childhood.

He grinned. "Well, as long as you're up, why don't you bring me some too."

I was surprised as he usually skips the sweets, while I am rather addicted to them.

When I returned with the two bowls of pudding, he asked, "So you're just going to chill out this afternoon?"

"Yeah, I'm into a good book. How about you?"

"The Men's Group has a speaker this afternoon. He's talking about the early days of the textile industry in Guilford City. Since it's all gone overseas, I'd like to know more about the time when it was one of the leading industries here."

So after finishing our pudding Ty headed for the Multi-Purpose Room where most programs are held, and I returned to my third floor apartment in the west wing. Sweetie, my tortoiseshell cat, greeted me at the door begging for a treat. I'm afraid I've spoiled her rotten, and I'm going to have to watch her weight. I wondered briefly if that would inspire me to watch my own.

I was deep into a Louise Penny mystery when the phone rang. It was the receptionist at the front desk.

"Ms. Weatherspoon?"

"Yes?"

"I have your name down as a volunteer guide on the weekends. Are you available this afternoon?"

The Marketing Department had recruited some of us to serve in their place on weekends if someone wanders in and wants a tour. I'd done it a couple of times and enjoyed showing off our facility to potential residents because I'm proud of it. We've never had a full house. In spite of the growing older population, the downturn in the economy, which prevented retirees from selling their homes, has had an impact on recruiting newcomers. Our building was constructed just prior to the collapse of the housing market, so it has been a constant struggle to sell apartments. And just as soon as three new residents move in, four might move to assisted living or the nursing unit or die, so those in our Marketing Department are some of the hardest working staff we have.

I told her I'd be happy to lead a tour and would be right down.

Kaylee, our weekend receptionist, introduced me to the attractive lady waiting for the tour.

"This is Mrs. Rinehart," she said. She turned to the visitor and said, "Ms. Weatherspoon will show you around. If you're interested in more information I have brochures here at the desk you can take with you when you leave."

The visitor smiled and put out her hand to shake mine. "Please call me Leah."

She was petite with ash blond hair that was either her natural color or had been done at a good salon. Her green eyes exuded good humor and her lovely smile made me like her immediately. She was dressed in a stylish jacketed dress in turquoise, and she even wore hose on this god-awful hot day. I wear only slacks now making panty hose a thing of the past, one of the perks of old age I guess.

"I'm Vi," I said.

I took her on the prescribed tour of dining room, library, craft shop, gift shop, exercise room, pool and spa, though we couldn't get into the multi-purpose room since the men's group was convened there. We ended up in the café having a cup of coffee together. The longer I was with her the more I liked her.

"Are you from around here?" I asked as we drank coffee and chatted.

"Yes, I'm from Guilford City. On the northwest side. How about you?"

"Oh, I'm from New England. But my only relative, a niece, lives in town. Quite a few people here come from out of state because they have children or other relatives nearby."

"That makes sense. They want to be near their kids but not impose on them."

"Do you have children?"

"Scattered far and wide, I'm afraid. But I love it here and don't want to leave."

"I was wondering, is there a Mister Rinehart?" I asked. I didn't mean to pry, but I thought it unusual she came alone if her husband was still living. However husbands are sometimes more reluctant to take the step to move into a retirement center, and if that were the case it could make it difficult for her to convince him it was the right thing to do.

"Mister Rinehart is long gone," she said.

Long gone? I wondered. *From this world or just from her?*

She must have noticed a look of confusion on my face because she said, "He split from me a few years ago. He married his secretary. How's that for a cliché?" She laughed. I could tell she'd gotten over whatever anger or grief she'd suffered at the time.

"Well, there are plenty of single women here. You'd feel right at home. They're divorced, widowed, or have always been single—like me."

She grinned. "How about single men? Are there many of them?"

"About a third of our population is male. I'd say about half of those are single. Most have been married and are widowers, but there are several who've always been single like my friend Ty Landowski."

Leah set her coffee cup down and looked at me wide-eyed.

"Is something wrong?" I asked.

"It just dawned on me. I know who you are. You and Mr. Landowski are the ones who solved the case of the man who got killed here."

To my great consternation the local paper had published a feature story about the murder of a resident in the spring and the fact that Ty and I had pursued the killer on our own. The police had arrested his wife for his murder, but Ty and I were convinced she was innocent, and we had managed to prove it. I was terribly worried the ensuing publicity would have a detrimental effect on Glendon Hills, but the fact the case was solved satisfactorily seemed to allay any fears. At least that was my perception. From what I could tell people seemed intrigued by the fact two old geezers could outsmart the police.

I wondered if I was wrong about this and she was going to bring up all sorts of issues about the safety of our campus.

"Guilty as charged," I said. I felt as though I was blushing even though I'm not the blushing type.

"That was fantastic!" she raved. "I couldn't believe you could outsmart the cops. I hadn't given Glendon Hills much thought as a place to retire to, but after reading that article I thought I'd like to go where such clever people live."

To say I was surprised is an understatement. I felt as

though I'd been absolved. I would be crushed to think the reputation of Glendon Hills had been hurt in any way.

"I'm quite relieved to hear that," I said. "I love this place, and I wouldn't do anything to hurt it. The staff has always been security minded, but they've taken even more steps to make sure everyone is protected. You wouldn't have to worry for a minute about your safety."

"I'm sure I wouldn't."

I liked Leah from the start but now I liked her even more. She obviously had an open mind and didn't make snap judgments.

"Would you like to see an apartment?" I asked. I would do whatever I could to ensure this woman became one of my neighbors. "The model apartment isn't open on weekends, but I'd be glad to show you mine. You have to realize I haven't gussied it up like the professionals did in the model, but if you can overlook the underwhelming décor, it would give you an idea of what the apartments are like."

"That's very sweet of you." She reached out and touched my arm. "Are you sure I wouldn't be intruding?"

"Of course not. I volunteered to help out marketing, and this is part of the job."

"Well, I really am curious to see one."

"Let's go on up then."

I led the way through the halls and we took up the elevator to my floor.

"Do you need a compass to get around?" she asked laughing as we stepped out on the third floor.

"No, you'd get the hang of it very soon. It does seem confusing at first, but it's actually laid out pretty simply."

We'd reached my door and I unlocked it and gestured for Leah to enter. Of course Sweetie was there to greet us. She's never shy, even though she's a rescued cat.

"What a beautiful cat!" Leah exclaimed. "Right now

I'm in a place where I can't have one, but if I move here, that's one of the first things I'll do. I'll go to the shelter and adopt a stray."

"You won't regret it," I said. "She's a wonderful companion. I don't understand retirement homes that don't allow pets."

"It's one of the reasons I'm interested in Glendon Hills." She looked around my kitchen and living/dining room that are open to each other with only a four-foot high wall dividing them. "This is very nice," she said. "The kitchen has nice appliances and plenty of cupboards. And you probably don't do much cooking."

"One of my favorite perks is that someone else prepares the meals. I only make my own breakfast and once in a while a sandwich and bowl of soup for lunch. The microwave is my best friend."

"Are the meals good here?"

"Does the fact I've put on thirty pounds tell you anything?"

Leah chuckled. "Good thing I'm forewarned. I'm always struggling with weight too."

That seemed hard to believe as tiny as she was.

"And your living room is a nice size too. Plenty of space for a roomy couch, a couple of chairs, and a table to eat at."

"More than adequate," I added.

"Oh, look! You have a balcony! How wonderful." Leah strode over to the door that leads out onto my six-by-twelve foot balcony overlooking the woods behind GH and opened the door before I could warn her or react. Sweetie streaked across the room, out the door and jumped onto a chair and then a table. It was if she'd waited all her life for this golden opportunity to explore the wide open spaces.

"No, Sweetie!" I shouted running after her. But by the time I reached the door, she put her forepaws on the balcony railing and propelled herself over the edge. I thought my heart would stop. I live on the third floor. I ran to the railing and looked down. There is a small bump-out on the first floor with a flat roof and she was perched near the edge looking a little stunned. Suddenly she plunged from the roof and landed on the ground, staggering slightly for a minute before sitting down to take stock of her situation.

Leah ran up beside me. "Oh, my god. I'm so sorry; I'm so sorry. I never thought…" Her voice broke and she looked absolutely devastated.

I pointed to Sweetie on the ground. She wasn't visibly injured. "Cats are pretty resilient," I said trying not to look as distressed as I felt. I was worried sick she'd broken something or been hurt internally. I didn't say this to Leah but I never let her out on the balcony because I'd always been afraid this would happen. She's so inquisitive and active I never trusted her. I made sure she was nowhere near when I stepped out on the balcony and closed the door behind me, and on less humid and hot days I had a roller screen I could pull across to let in fresh air but keep her in the apartment. Unfortunately the roller screen was rolled up.

"This is terrible," Leah continued, distraught. "Can we go down and get her?"

"Why don't you keep an eye on her in case she gets up and runs off, and I'll go down to the first floor and hope she's still there when I get outside. If she does take off, let me know which way she went."

I left an upset Leah, raced down the steps to the bottom floor, and went out of the door from the community room. But there was no Sweetie in sight. I didn't know whether to be crushed or happy. At least it meant she was able to move on her own so hopefully she wasn't severely injured. But would I ever find her again?

TWO

BACK IN MY apartment Leah was sitting on a chair on the balcony, her head in her hands. She looked up when I came in. Tears had made tracks down her cheeks.

"At least she can move," she said shakily. "She got up and stood there for a minute as though assessing the damage then ran straight into the woods. I guess that means she wasn't badly hurt." She wiped away the tears with a tissue. "Let me help you look for her."

"That's not necessary," I said. Leah was not only dressed in her Sunday best but wore high heels. The woods behind GH have heavy undergrowth. There was no way she could make it in those shoes.

"It is," she said. "You can't imagine how horrible I feel about this. I'll never have any peace of mind unless I can try to make up for my stupidity."

I went over and took her hand in mind. "That was simply an unfortunate accident. You couldn't have known what a crazy cat I have."

"I'm serious, Vi. I insist on helping."

I pointed at her shoes. "You'd never make it in the woods in those."

"Do you have anything I can borrow?"

"I have big clodhopper feet," I said. "Yours look pretty dainty. Size six?"

"Actually seven."

"Well, I wear nine You'd swim in them."

"We can stuff the toes with toilet paper. I'm not backing down." This little lady could be very emphatic and she spoke with authority.

"What about your nice dress? The branches would probably tear it."

"Let me borrow some sweat pants and T-shirt. Whatever old thing you've got."

Leah was nothing if not determined. I didn't want to spend the afternoon arguing with her; I wanted to get out there as soon as possible to look for Sweetie so I gave in. I pulled out some stretchy pants that had a pull string around the waist. Good thing because she was about four sizes smaller than I am. I found an old T-shirt and sneakers and gave them all to her.

While she was in the bathroom changing, I quickly exchanged my clothing for the lightest weight exercise clothes I could find: grey cotton pants and T-shirt that said "Girl Scouts Know How the Cookie Crumbles."

She came out ten minutes later looking like a waif in the oversize clothing that hung on her frame. The UNC T-shirt hung nearly to her knees, and she had the pants rolled up so they wouldn't trail on the ground. I couldn't help but smile even though I was sick at heart over Sweetie.

"I wish I had a camera," I said. "Your friends would never know you. Can you manage okay?"

"The shoes don't feel too bad with paper stuffed in the toes," she said. "Come on, let's go before your cat gets too far."

We went down the elevator and out the door in the community room, and Leah pointed ahead to the wooded area.

"She went into the woods about there," she said. "I remember that tree that's half fallen over."

I knew that the Glendon Hills property ended a couple hundred yards away. It butts up against an area that is part of a county park that covers several hundred acres. We love it because it means nothing will ever be built behind us to ruin our lovely view. But now it meant a huge area of thick forest that could conceal Sweetie and be very dangerous for her. I'd had a chip put in to identify her should some stranger find her, but that possibility seemed remote out here.

Leah followed me gamely into the woods. Even though I'm seventy-six, I'm still in good shape. Being an executive director of a Girl Scout council means you often participate in challenges along with the girls, so I'm probably more physically active than many people my age. Leah, because of her short legs, had to hustle to keep up with me.

I'd gathered up a walking stick and a can of orange spray paint while she was changing her clothes. I'd bought the paint in the fall to make a Halloween costume for a GH party. I hadn't dressed up for Halloween since I was a kid, but I decided to abandon my inhibitions and went as a giant cardboard pumpkin, wearing it like a sandwich-board sign with straps over the shoulders. It won second place in the costume contest. My claim to fame.

I put the paint and a couple of bottles of water into an old backpack I'd used for trips. I didn't know how long we'd be out in the woods and we didn't want to get dehydrated on such a hot day.

I took my cell phone along as well in case my tracking skills had gotten rusty. I wasn't sure if GPS, which I could access on my phone, would work out in the woods, but I could always call for help if we became hopelessly lost.

We called Sweetie's name as we laboriously made our way through the underbrush. Every few feet I would tag a tree with a spot of orange paint so we could find our way back.

Even though the thick tree cover gave us shade, the air was hot and humid and prevented any stray breeze from reaching us. It wasn't long before both of us were soaked with sweat. I wished I'd tied a rag around my head to keep it from running into my eyes. When I found a fallen log, I urged Leah to sit down with me for a few minutes.

"We don't need to get a heat stroke," I said. I handed her a bottle and took a sip of water from my own. "It would be tough to find us out here." I pulled the phone out of my pocket. "By the way, I want you to know I have this. I believe they can track us through the phone in an emergency."

"Maybe you should go back home," Leah said. "I'd feel even worse than I do already if anything happened to you. I can keep looking by myself."

"No way. I would never leave you out here alone." I looked at my watch. "It's four-twenty-seven. Let's look until five. If we haven't found her by then we'll go back."

"Only if you promise to go sooner if you start feeling bad."

"I promise. Same for you."

We trudged onward, calling Sweetie's name. I knew it was probably a lost cause in such a huge expanse of woods, but I needed to make an effort to find her. Poor little Sweetie. I didn't know if she would ever find her way back home. She'd never been out of my apartment since I adopted her except to go to the vet's. It wasn't like living in a house where a cat is used to going in and out. Would she ever recognize our big building as "home?"

It was nearly five when we came upon a small ravine made by a meandering creek.

"Something smells really awful," Leah said.

I took a deep breath. She was right; it was pretty bad. "I'd guess there's a dead animal around here somewhere. Maybe a raccoon or even a deer. Let's head back. We're not going to find her today."

"I'm all for it. But can I soak my feet in the water for a few minutes first? They're killing me. I'll have to admit wearing shoes two sizes too large is not the brightest thing I've ever done."

"That bank looks a little steep," I said.

We worked our way carefully down the bank to the water's edge. The stream curved sharply a hundred feet or so to our right.

"I'm going around that bend and see if there's a rock or log I can sit on," Leah said. "It's pretty muddy here."

"I'm right behind you."

I followed her as she made her way along the uneven root-filled bank in search of a seating area.

We'd just gone around the curve when suddenly she stopped dead in her tracks.

"Oh, my god," she said, pointing in front of her.

I couldn't see what she was pointing at so I stepped up beside her.

Sprawled in an unnatural twisted position beside the water was a man, face turned toward the ground and his hair matted with blood. He was dressed in jeans and T-shirt and Nikes. One arm was thrown out toward the stream and his fingers bobbed in the moving water. He looked very dead to me.

Leah rushed to his side and picked up his arm and felt his wrist.

She turned to me and shook her head. "No pulse," she said. "I'm going to try CPR."

"You have a medical background?" I asked.

"I was a nurse years ago." She got down on her hands and knees and took his head and gently turned it face up. His body flopped over so he was half on his back. His face was puffy, and I could see some maggots along the hairline. I'd never seen anything like that when we did our disaster training at the Girl Scout camp. I realized now how far from reality that exercise was. Ketchup is not the same as blood. And maggots bring an extra dose of authenticity I could have done without.

She dropped back and looked at him in horror and covered her face with her hands. She mumbled something I couldn't understand.

"What?" I asked.

She took away her hands. "I think I know him. His face is so distorted it's hard to tell, but I think it's Jeremy Scofield."

"Who's that?"

"He was a friend of my husband."

"It's too late for CPR isn't it?" I asked. That was so obviously true I don't know why I asked except I didn't want to accept the reality of it.

"Way too late. Apparently he's been in and out of rigor so it's been a while."

"Any idea what happened? Do you think he tripped and hit his head?"

"Whatever it was it didn't happen here."

"How can you tell?"

"His face would have been almost black because blood would have pooled in the lowest part of his body if he'd died here. Someone brought him here and dumped him."

My stomach was churning and I felt faint. But I didn't want Leah to worry about me too, so I sat down on a log and put my head between my knees.

"Are you all right?" Leah asked. She got up and came over beside me.

I raised my head. "Just a little light-headed. But I'll be okay." That wasn't totally true, but I wasn't going to tell her I was on the verge of losing my brunch. "The last time

I was close to a murder victim I didn't view the body, thank god. It's not a pretty sight."

"No, it's definitely not. Good thing you brought a phone, Vi. Let's call the cops."

I pulled the phone out of my pocket and dialed 9-1-1 praying I would get service. Thankfully it got through.

I explained to the dispatcher that we'd found a body and we were pretty far out in the woods.

"I don't know if you can locate us by triangulating on the cell phone or whatever it is you do, but I can give you a fairly simple way to find us. We went into the woods directly behind the largest building at Glendon Hills Retirement Center. Opposite the door to the community room. I tagged the trees with orange spray paint as we went along so someone could easily follow our trail."

The dispatcher said that help was on the way and asked us to wait until the police arrived so we could give them whatever information we knew.

"We'll be right here. But tell them to hurry. We're about to wilt in this heat."

After I hung up and put the phone back in my pocket I noticed Leah looking at me with a strange expression.

"Something the matter?" I asked and then realized what a really dumb question that was under the circumstances.

She gave me a fleeting but quirky smile and said, "Is there something about you that draws you to violent situations? I mean twice now in a few months is kind of spooky don't you think?"

I shrugged my shoulders. "I've gone for seventy-six years without ever running into anything remotely like this. I haven't a clue why it's happening now. I have to tell you it's freaking me out."

THREE

It took the police almost forty minutes to find us. In the meantime Leah and I retraced our steps into the woods away from the odor where we found a log to sit on. Neither of us was keen on sitting next to the poor dead man.

"You said you thought you knew him?" I asked her, once we had settled in.

"I'm pretty sure he's the guy who was once the morning anchor on Channel 6. But he got fired a couple of years ago. I guess that would be before you moved to Guilford City. It's hard to tell for sure because lying out here in the heat and all hasn't done him any good. Actually he was pretty good-looking."

"I didn't look at him for long since I was pretty grossed out. I'd be hard pressed to say he was handsome."

"Death has a way of doing that to you, especially a violent one. He and my ex used to be good friends."

The heat was really getting to me now so I pulled my bottle of water out of the backpack I'd thrown on the ground and took a good long swig. I handed Leah's bottle to her, and she drank as though we were on the Sahara Desert. I was so glad I'd brought them along because we were going to be here far longer than we thought.

"Used to be friends?" I asked after we were both satiated.

"They knew each other since University. And over the years they talked about going into business together. But it was all a lot of talk. Nothing ever came of it."

NANCY GOTTER GATES　　　23

"You said he got fired. Why was that?"

"He was driving drunk and hit a woman badly injuring her. Lucky for him she didn't die. But she spent quite a while in the hospital and ended up in a wheelchair."

"Oh, good lord. So what did he do after he was let go from the station?"

"Well, first he spent a few months in jail. When he got out my ex had pity on him and hired him. I'm not sure anyone else would have."

"What does your ex do?"

"He runs an advertising agency. I guess he thought Jeremy's experience in TV would be an asset."

"But you said they used to be friends. Did something happen?"

"Oh, yeah. Lawrence found out Jeremy was skimming money off the accounts. So he fired him a month or so ago."

"So there was bad blood between the two."

"Absolutely. Lawrence thought he was doing him a big favor by taking him on. Then to find out he was cheating him...well."

"That was a heck of a way to pay him back for his kindness," I said, brushing an inquisitive spider off my pants leg.

"Not only that, he was hitting on Deborah. That's his wife and secretary."

"Jeez."

Leah shook her head. "That's the kind of guy he was. I never liked him. I knew he was a drunk, and he thought he was God's gift to women. When I was still married to Lawrence we went out occasionally with Jeremy and his wife, but he used to flirt with me in front of her so I finally said I didn't want to socialize with them any more. After that the men would sometimes go out to bars together, but he never came to our house. That's why I said he was Lawrence's friend, not *our* friend."

We both fell into a meditative silence after that. The wait for the police seemed interminable. I knew it was going to take some time to follow our trail, but I wanted desperately to get this whole thing behind us. And I wanted to get back to our building to see if Sweetie had returned.

Finally the authorities showed up: two cops in uniform and a detective, I assumed, in slacks and shirt unbuttoned at the neck. He'd pulled loose his tie and carried his jacket over his arm. His shirt was soaked with sweat. Another man in casual dress carried a camera. At least the uniformed cops had short sleeves but their faces were flushed from the heat. There were two EMTs carrying a stretcher behind them.

We got to our feet as they approached.

The detective looked a little startled when he got up close.

"What are you two ladies doing way out here?" he asked. I knew he meant what are you ladies *at your advanced age* doing out here?

"I live at Glendon Hills," I said. "My cat ran away and we were trying to find her."

"You need to be careful or you'll get a heat stroke," he said frowning. "You shouldn't be out here on a day like this."

"We brought water along. We're doing okay. But we are anxious to get back."

"I'll try not to keep you long then. Show me what you found."

Leah led the way back to the bank of the creek to where the body lay. The EMTs quickly went to him and determined he was indeed dead, as if there was any doubt.

As soon as they determined he was deceased, the man with the camera began taking shots of him from all angles.

"Why don't we go back to where you were waiting for us, and I'll ask you a few questions. By the way I'm Detective Fentress."

I was relieved he didn't make us stay at the crime scene. My tolerance for the odor and the heat had just about reached its limit.

We asked if we could sit down, we were pretty weary at this point, and we settled back on the log while Fentress remained standing. It was intimidating to have him towering over us, but I was too tired and hot to care. Since it was so obvious the body had been there for a while, he couldn't possibly consider us suspects.

"First I need your personal information," he said.

We gave him our names, addresses, phone numbers and so on. When that was done he asked us to recount how we discovered the body.

Leah told him how she went around the bend of the creek to find a place where she could sit and soak her feet.

She grinned for a minute, a respite from the grimness of the occasion. "I had to borrow shoes two sizes too big from Vi here. I was wearing heels and knew I couldn't make it in the woods with those."

"Are you two friends?" he asked.

"We just met," I said. "I was showing her around Glendon Hills because she's thinking about moving here. When my cat ran off, she insisted on helping me look for her."

"I see. Back to finding the body. Was it laying the way it is now?"

"No," Leah said. "I'm a former nurse. When I first saw him I thought maybe I could give him CPR. He was lying facedown, so I turned him over. But then I realized he'd been dead a while. I hope I didn't mess up the crime scene."

Fentress smiled at that. "You must be a fan of cop shows."

"I am. And from my nurse's training I have to tell you I don't think he died here."

"Why is that?"

"Because he was facedown and the blood didn't pool there."

Fentress nodded his head as he noted that down. "Good observation. Anything else you can tell me, either of you?"

We both shook our heads.

"I'm going to have one of the patrolmen walk you back to the building. I don't want to keep you out here any longer in this heat. But I might need to contact you later with more questions."

We were so relieved to be leaving. I felt that I had just about enough energy left to get home, and then I would collapse for sure.

It took us twenty-five minutes to return to the edge of the forest. Much as I love the woods, I was never so happy to see grass in my life. I felt like falling to my knees and kissing it. But I knew if I did, I'd never be able to get up again.

The patrolman delivered us to the door of the community room and then returned to the woods. I didn't envy him having to make that trek another couple of times.

Before going in I looked all around the back of the building, but there was no sign of Sweetie.

"She'll probably come back when she gets real hungry. Never saw a cat who loves to eat the way she does," I said with more conviction than I felt.

Leah began to tear up again. "I'll never forgive myself."

I put my arm around her shoulder. "Nonsense. As I said before, it was an accident. Don't beat yourself up."

She wiped her eyes. "What a day."

"What a day," I echoed.

I used my pass card to open the door, and Leah and I limped up to my apartment. I gave her a fresh washcloth and towel and told her she could take a shower if she wished. I got out the shampoo and hair dryer for her as I knew her head had been soaked with sweat. I'd take my turn when she was done. In the meantime I lounged in my recliner, which I'd covered with a sheet so I wouldn't get dirt and sweat on the upholstery, and almost fell asleep.

Leah came out looking refreshed but was carrying her high heels in her hand.

"My feet hurt too much to wear these," she said. "I'm going to have to drive barefoot."

"Can you sit a minute and have a glass of ice tea?" I asked. "I'd offer you dinner but I have next to nothing in my fridge. And they don't serve supper downstairs on Sunday evenings."

"Don't you want to shower?"

"That can wait a few minutes. I have a couple of questions to ask you."

She looked at me quizzically but said, "Sure. Iced tea sounds good."

I poured us each a glass and we sat at my dining table.

"Okay, so what did you want to ask?" Leah said after taking a large swig.

"I noticed you never mentioned to the cop that you thought you knew the victim."

"He never asked me."

"Well I suppose it never occurred to him you might know him. But I was surprised you didn't volunteer the information."

She pursed her lips. "I thought about it. But then I thought about his relationship with Lawrence. I didn't want to put any ideas in their heads since they'd had a falling-out."

"I kind of thought that might be the case."

She shrugged. "They'll probably find out anyway. But I didn't want to be the one to point them in that direction."

"But Leah," I said. "don't you think it's going to look a little strange when they find out you knew him but didn't mention it to them?"

Her mouth dropped open and she looked stricken. "Oh, my god, Vi. What have I done?"

FOUR

I HADN'T THOUGHT to check my phone messages until Leah had left and I'd taken my own shower. But I did so now.

"Where the heck are you, Vi?" It was Ty sounding very anxious. "If I don't hear from you in the next hour I'm going to send security up to check your apartment." It had been recorded thirty-five minutes earlier. He must have called just before I got home.

Tyrone Landowski and I first met when we both moved here about a year ago; I came from Maine and a career with the Girl Scouts while Ty had lived all over the world working with the State Department. My reason for choosing GH was because my only relative, my niece Greta, and her husband live nearby. She's my late sister's daughter and my only living relative. They were kind enough to ask me to live with them, but I had no intention of imposing upon them. However, I thought it would be nice to be close to them in my retirement, and I also was glad to leave the frozen winters of Maine behind.

Ty ended up here, he says, because he wanted someplace where he could enjoy all four seasons (even if it could get as scorching as it was today or miserably cold in winter). He thought it was a nice compromise between Florida and New England. Maybe we bonded because neither of us had ever married (and aren't interested in doing so at this late date), or maybe we saw our own stubborn and opinionated selves reflected in each other. But we are so in tune that I feel that he's the brother I never had.

The other thing we have in common is loathing our given names. My mother named me Viola after her (misplaced) love of the instrument she played with disastrous results. So I go by Vi which seems a little less saccharine. Poor Ty's mother had a crush on the popular movie star of her day, Tyrone Power, so he's endured so many questions as to why a Polish boy would have such an unlikely first name.

Ty and I had planned to go out to Panera's for supper. He lives on the East Wing and I live on the West so we usually meet in the lobby if we are going out. I knew I would have been frantic if Ty hadn't shown up. I called him back immediately. It was six-forty-two, nearly forty-five minutes later than we agreed to meet.

"Vi?!" he answered. I realized he saw my name on Caller ID. "I've been worried about you. You're usually so prompt. Are you okay?"

"I'm pooped but hungry. Why don't we talk about it over dinner?"

"Okay. I'll see you in the lobby." I heard relief in his voice. I hated that he'd been upset over my absence, but I'll admit it felt good to know somebody cared that much.

I wouldn't tell him anything until we were settled in at the restaurant with our bowls of soup. It's a short drive to Panera's, and I didn't want to get started on the tale only to be interrupted when we had to stand in line to order our food.

I could tell Ty was agitated by the grim look on his face and the fact he kept running his hand through his wiry gray curls. He isn't always the most patient of men.

When we were settled in at last, I began my tale by explaining I'd been asked to show Leah around Glendon Hills.

"I didn't know you volunteered to give tours," he said.

"I've done it once or twice before. It's fun to show off our place."

"Did you tell her we call it 'Geezer Heaven'?"

I shook my head. "No, Ty. I didn't think she'd appreciate our brand of humor. Now, do you want me to tell you what happened or not?"

Chastened, he gestured with his spoon and said, "Go on."

When I got to the part about Sweetie jumping off the balcony, he put his spoon down and said, "My god, Vi, did it kill her?" He had quite a soft spot for my cat.

"No, she landed on the roof of the first floor bump-out and was stunned for a minute, but then she jumped to the ground and ran off into the woods."

"Has she come back?"

"Not yet."

We both took a moment to mourn her disappearance. Now that I said it out loud a wave of melancholy swept over me and I felt my eyes tear up. I used my napkin to wipe them away.

"I'm so sorry, Vi. But surely she'll be back." He looked as stricken as I felt.

"I don't know, Ty. It's not like she's ever been outside here. She probably doesn't know where 'home' is."

"So when did this happen?"

I looked at my watch. "About three-and-a-half hours ago."

"You've been looking for her all this time?"

"Kind of. But let me tell you the rest of the story."

So I explained how I gave Leah clothes appropriate for hiking in the woods and we took off to look for Sweetie.

Ty scowled. "That wasn't too smart. Those woods go a long way back. What if you two had gotten lost? That could have been very dangerous, especially on such a hot day."

"I've done my share of hiking with the Girl Scouts. I'm not totally naïve. I took a can of spray paint to mark the trees and my cell phone in case we got in trouble."

"But this heat…"

"We had bottled water. 'Always Be Prepared.' That doesn't just apply to the Boy Scouts, you know." I was getting annoyed with him. It seemed he had no faith in my judgment.

He bit his lip. "Sorry. It's just that I worry about you. Didn't mean to imply you don't have good sense."

"It sounded like it," I growled.

He massaged his forehead with his fingertips then slouched back in his chair. "I'm not trying to pick a fight. I want to hear the rest of it."

I sighed. "I know that. I'm just so upset over Sweetie, and it's been a hell of a day."

I continued my story about tramping through the woods and finally coming to the creek.

"We were going to turn back, but Leah's feet were hurting, and she wanted to soak them in the water for a few minutes before we left."

"You said she was wearing your shoes, and they were two sizes two big? No wonder they hurt! How bright was that?"

I glared at him as fiercely as I could. One more remark like that, and I wasn't going to tell him the rest of the story. I felt like a sulky five-year-old.

He immediately realized he was treading on quicksand. He put his hand to his mouth. "Oops, sorry."

I scowled for another minute to make sure he got the message. Finally I told him about going around the bend of the creek and finding the body.

His mouth dropped open. "Again?"

I didn't care if he spoke as long as it wasn't some snide remark.

"Well, I didn't really 'find' Ralph Duncan. You and I just happened upon his wife with the bloody knife in her hand. In fact I never did see Ralph's body. I wish I hadn't seen this one. It wasn't a pretty sight."

"I imagine not. So what did you do?"

"Leah was a nurse. He was lying facedown, and she turned him over thinking she could do CPR. But it was immediately obvious he was dead."

"Good thing you had your phone."

"Right. I was afraid it might not work out there in the woods, but it did, thank god. But it took the cops about forty minutes to follow our trail and find us."

"So what happened then?"

"They questioned us, of course. But there wasn't much we could tell them of course. They said they might get back to us sometime later."

"How did Leah handle all this?"

"Not too well. Of course she was distraught at letting Sweetie out on the balcony. And then finding the body. It certainly wasn't a very good day for her. But I am concerned about her."

"Why is that?"

"Apparently she knew the victim, or at least who he was. But she didn't tell the cops that."

"Why not for Pete's sake?"

"He was a former TV anchor in town who lost his job a couple of years ago when he hit a woman while he was driving drunk. He spent some months in jail for that. When he got out, Leah's ex-husband hired him for his advertising agency. They'd been pals in the past."

"So? What's the big deal with that?"

"He caught this guy, Jeremy, stealing from him so

he fired him and there's a lot of bad blood there. I don't think she dislikes her former husband enough to cast any suspicion on him. She didn't want to be the one to open Pandora's box."

"But she could get in trouble when they find out she knew him and didn't tell them."

"Exactly what I told her."

"Oh, boy," said Ty.

FIVE

I WAS TOO tired to stay up and see if the murder was on the late night news. All that tromping around in the heat really did me in. But it was on the local news the next morning. I watched the station where Jeremy had once been anchor to see how they reported it.

It was the lead story. "Former Channel 6 evening anchor, Jeremy Scofield, was found dead yesterday afternoon by two hikers in dense woods at Liberty Park," the current anchor reported. "It was some distance from any parking lot or road, and Guilford City police say the body might have laid there for months or years except for the fact the two local women, Leah Rinehart and Viola Weatherspoon, were searching for a runaway cat. The police estimate the time of death as sometime late Friday night or early Saturday. They did not state the cause of death but are treating it as suspicious.

"Scofield was charged with DUI and reckless driving when he hit and badly injured a woman in 2008 and was incarcerated for eight months. Following his release he was employed by Rinehart Advertising Agency, but Channel 6 has learned that he was recently fired from that job.

"No other information about the investigation is available at this time."

Oh god. I wish our names hadn't been publicly announced.

A few minutes later my phone rang, and it was Ty.

"I was listening to the news. Sounds like the cat is

already out of the bag," he said. "I think your friend Leah is going to have some explaining to do."

I sighed. "Yeah. She's not really my friend. I didn't know her before yesterday. But it sounds as if she's going to need some good friends very soon."

After I ate a bite of breakfast—my usual: cereal, banana and coffee—I dressed and went outside to walk the perimeter of the building. As I walked along the edge of the woods at the back of the building I called out, "Here, Sweetie. Come get some treats." I'd put a handful in a pocket in case I spied her, but all I heard was the occasional call of a bird and the rustling sound of squirrels running through the underbrush. I was heartsick at the thought she might never return home. But I made up my mind I wasn't going to give up hope so soon. After all, cats have minds of their own.

I went to water aerobics at ten hoping no one had seen the early morning news, but I wasn't that fortunate.

Cora Lee Hillman, the resident gossip, was in the locker room changing into her swimsuit when I arrived. The last person I wanted to discuss it with.

"Well, Vi, I see you're at it again. You must have an affinity for dead bodies."

"I don't think so, Cora. This is the first one I've ever seen. And I sincerely hope the last."

"What about Ralph Duncan?"

"I never saw him. I only tried to help Phyllis."

"Well, I must say you keep things interesting around here."

"I think things are plenty interesting without my help. Well, I've got to go shower."

I'd already taken a shower in my apartment, but I wanted to get away from her "inquiring mind."

Apparently no one else in the class had seen the early

news, and Cora Lee hadn't yet had the chance to spread the word. Spunky, our instructor, kept us moving at a pace that didn't allow any talking. Afterwards, I usually spend a few minutes in the hot tub/spa, but today I rushed out of there before Cora Lee could engage me in further conversation.

After I got back to my apartment I checked for messages on my phone as usual. I found one short plaintive message.

"It's Leah Rinehart, Vi. You were right. I should have told the cops that I knew who the dead person was. A couple of detectives came out to my house this morning to question me again. They'd learned about Jeremy's connection with Lawrence and apparently they are considering him a person of interest. They wanted to know why I never mentioned the fact he'd worked for my ex-husband and they'd known each other for years. I told them I didn't recognize him, but I don't think they really bought that. I should have left him facedown. Then they might have believed me. Can we get together and talk? You were involved in something like this before. Can you give me some advice?"

I called her back.

"I'll be happy to talk to you, Leah, but I don't know what I can do."

"I'd just feel so much better if I had someone I could discuss this with. I'm not anxious to let my friends know about this, and I don't have any family near by. Please?"

"Well, if it will give you any comfort. Could we include my friend Ty? He might have some ideas."

"Sure. I'm afraid I can use all the help I can get. Since I'd like our talk to be private, how about the two of you coming over here?"

"When would you like us to come? I'll have to see what plans Ty has."

"The sooner the better. Could you come this afternoon?"

"Let me check with Ty and get back to you."

Ty was going to play cards with the Bridge Dudes, something he does regularly when there's nothing else on his schedule, but he said he could get a substitute, and we decided to go to Leah's house after lunch. She was happy and relieved when I called her back with our plans.

We drove to Leah's house in Ty's cute two-seater red convertible. It can be one hundred in the shade, and Ty will always put the top down. He adores driving with the wind in his face even if that wind feels like it's coming out of a blast furnace. So I put on the pink sequined ball cap he keeps in the car for me in an attempt to shield my face from the blistering sun. Sunblock alone just isn't enough.

Leah lived in a condo development on the other side of Guilford City. She'd told me on our tramp through the woods that when her marriage broke up she'd moved out of their large home in Nathan Park where my niece lives.

"I didn't need all that space, and frankly it held some unpleasant memories. I was glad to turn it over to Lawrence and his new wife."

Her condo wasn't exactly tiny. Located in one of the newer upscale developments it must have been more than two thousand square feet.

"So you're the famous Ty Landowski," Leah said when she greeted us at the door and I introduced them.

Ty laughed. "Infamous maybe."

"Well, you and Vi made somewhat of a splash locally when that man was killed at Glendon Hills."

"Well, we just sort of stumbled into that one. We certainly hadn't set out to play detective. But when they arrested his wife we knew we had to do something."

"You did considerably more than 'something,'" Leah said. "You rescued her from a lifetime in jail."

"More likely a mental institution," I said. "They were trying to say she was mentally unbalanced."

"Either one would have been terrible," Leah replied as she led us into the living room where Ty and I sat on the down-filled pale green sofa. I detected a designer's touch in the impeccable furnishings that were obviously pricey but had an inviting, homey feel. There was nothing ostentatious about the décor.

"Coffee, tea?"

We both asked for coffee. I knew it was probably a mistake to drink it after lunch as I would no doubt have trouble going to sleep that night. But when faced with difficult discussions or decisions, it is always my drug of choice.

We had an opportunity to admire the room and its many eclectic touches like the side chairs upholstered in a deep green ikat pattern and the variety of intriguing tchotchkes on the built-in bookcases flanking the fireplace faced in gold glass tiles. I wondered how she would ever be able to give up any of these beautiful objects to downsize to a GH apartment. We did have a couple of sizeable apartments at the end of each wing that would probably be her choice.

Leah was soon back carrying a tray with three cups of coffee along with cream and sugar bowls which she set on the glass-topped coffee table.

"Love this individual coffee brewing system. Makes it so easy to make a quick cup," she said.

I thought of my ancient percolator that was older than Methuselah. Of course I rarely used it since I could always get a quick cup in our café.

"I'm so glad Vi invited you along," Leah said to Ty. "You seem to be a pretty good team."

Ty smiled broadly. "I guess that's a good way to put it. We're the Mutt and Jeff of Glendon Hills."

"So what can we do for you?" I asked. "You surely don't

think you're under suspicion do you? I mean because you didn't tell the police that you knew who the victim was."

"No, I don't think so." She thought for a minute and added, "Unless they could construe it that I was an accessory after the fact because I didn't identify him."

Ty looked pained. "Mmmm. I guess that's a possibility. But, after all, you guys did report finding a body. It's not like you were trying to hide it."

She nodded thoughtfully. "True. But my main concern is Lawrence. You know, for a long time I harbored a lot of anger toward him. I couldn't believe he left me for his younger secretary. But after a lot of soul searching I had to admit to myself that I wasn't the best wife ever. I'd always been interested in art and after the kids grew up and went away to University I got very involved in the art world. I became a docent at the university art museum and a member of just about every art organization in town. I was so busy with all of that I really neglected Lawrence. I was seldom available to him. It's no wonder he turned to someone else."

"Are you a painter?" I asked.

"Only in the most amateurish way. I dabble at it, but I'll never be any good. For a time there I took lessons and thought I could turn into a real artist. But I just don't have the talent. But I deluded myself for a long time over my ability. Such a fool." She shook her head.

"Back to Lawrence," Ty piped up. "Do you think the police have zeroed in on him as a suspect?"

"I'm worried that's a good possibility. The timing for one thing—the fact it happened so soon after Lawrence fired Jeremy. You'd think it would seem more logical that Jeremy would want to hurt Lawrence than the other way around. But I'm wondering if they had a confrontation that got out of hand. Maybe a scuffle where Lawrence pushed Jeremy and he hit his head on something."

"Have you talked to him at all? Does he have an alibi?" I asked.

She bit her lip and shook her head. "I called their house last night. Deborah, his wife, told me Lawrence went out of town to a conference Saturday morning and wasn't back yet. I told her what happened, and she was shocked of course. I asked if Lawrence had seen Jeremy lately and she said she didn't think so. At least he hadn't said anything about it."

"So he left Saturday morning," I said. "They said on TV that Jeremy could have been killed Friday night."

"Did she say where Lawrence was Friday night?" Ty asked.

"I didn't think to ask her. I had no idea about possible time of death when I talked to her."

"Well, I would guess a lot hinges on where he was on Friday," Ty said. "If he doesn't have an alibi, he might be in trouble."

"Did you know Jeremy well enough to know if he had any enemies?" I asked.

"Well of course there's always the family of the woman he hurt when he was driving drunk. I understand she's been in a wheelchair ever since."

"But that's been a while ago. Why wait till now for revenge?"

"Good question. Doesn't make much sense, does it? Lawrence knows far more about him than I do. I don't really know who his friends and/or enemies are…were."

"Sounds to me like there's nothing to be done at this point. If Lawrence is designated as a person of interest by the police, we might be able to look into it. But he might not even be under suspicion. Or if he is, maybe he can clear it all up when he comes home."

Leah looked sheepish. "I'm sorry," she said. "I guess I jumped the gun. I've just been so upset about it all. Especially when the police came back to interview me again. I'm so worried about Lawrence."

Ty rose. "You know we'd like to help you if we could," he said. "But let's hope it's unnecessary. Let's keep in touch and see how this all falls out."

Leah got up too. "You're so kind to come over. Sorry it turned out to be something of a wild goose chase."

"No problem," I said. "By the way, how are your feet?"

"My feet?"

"After wearing my clodhoppers through the woods. Do you have blisters all over your feet?"

She smiled and shrugged. "They're getting better. Remind me not to try that again, though."

Then she looked solemn again. "Has Sweetie come back?"

"Not yet."

She closed her eyes and shook her head. "I still feel terrible about that."

"Don't. It was just an accident." I didn't feel nearly as magnanimous as I tried to sound, but I hoped she didn't hear a false note in my reply.

On the way home, Ty said, "Do you think it's a little strange that she's so concerned about her ex, the guy who left her for someone else?"

"Yeah, I think there's a lot of remorse there. She admitted that she didn't treat him very well and probably drove him into the arms of his secretary."

"Well, most women would be pretty bitter. Don't quite understand the dynamics of their relationship. You know, Vi, the fact that neither of us married, maybe we're just out of touch with how these things work. I, at least, don't get it."

"Me neither." I wondered if she still had feelings for Lawrence. Some women don't feel complete unless they have a man in their lives. I presumed Leah was one of those.

SIX

EVERY MORNING I walked the perimeter of the building and along the edge of the woods hoping to find Sweetie. But there was no sign of her. I was getting more and more discouraged, afraid I'd never see her again.

I didn't hear from Leah again until Friday. She called me just before I went downstairs for dinner.

"I just found out that they've arrested Lawrence," she said. "We've got to do something, Vi."

"Oh I'm so sorry. Do you know any details?"

"I don't. Nor does Deborah. She called me, hysterical, and said he'd called from his office to tell her they were taking him in. He told her not to come down to the jail, but he would contact his lawyer to arrange bail. That's all she knows."

"Do you know who his lawyer is?"

"No idea."

I glanced at my watch. It was just about five o'clock. "Let me turn on the local news and see if I can learn anything."

I hung up and turned on the TV. Sure enough the story was at the top of the news.

"Lawrence Rinehart, president of Rinehart Advertising Agency, has been arrested by the Guilford City Police for the murder of Jeremy Scofield who once anchored the early news at this station. Scofield's body was found last Sunday by two women in Liberty Park in a heavily wooded area. Scofield was hired by Mr. Rinehart after he was released from jail two years ago following his in-carceration for DUI. He hit a woman seriously injuring her and spent eight months behind bars. Channel 6 has learned that Scofield was fired from his job at the agency in March, but the details of his firing have not been made public. The police have not released any further information on the arrest."

That wasn't very enlightening. I hurried downstairs because I knew that Ty would be waiting for me. Unsurprisingly Ty was frowning when I got to the lobby.

"You okay?" he asked.

"Quit being such a worrywart. Of course I'm okay. I just waited to look at the beginning of the early news."

"Any special reason?"

"I'll tell you after we get waited on. Let's go get a table."

Since patience isn't one of his virtues, Ty fiddled with the silverware and salt and pepper shakers while waiting for our meals to come. I wasn't trying to torture him, but wanted to keep our conversation confidential. I was afraid if any of the wait staff got a whiff of what we would be talking about the word would get out quickly. Since the diners are the same people day after day, there's a lot of camaraderie between the dining room staff and the residents. They're a part of our big GH family, and I'm not sure they're above being as gossipy as everyone else.

Finally we were served. I'd ordered one of my favorites, Moravian chicken pie filled with big chunks of white meat chicken and lots of sauce with a flaky shell. Not exactly low cal. I felt virtuous ordering green peas to go with it. Ty had salmon, stewed okra, and a small salad.

Ty gave a huge sigh. "Okay, we're alone. Tell me what's going on."

"Leah's ex-husband has been arrested for Jeremy Scofield's murder."

"Well, I guess that's not too surprising. Any details? What do they have on him?"

"They're saying very little. Leah called me just before five to tell me. That's why I was late. I wanted to see what was on the early news, but they didn't give any real information. Leah doesn't know anything either. She's terribly upset though."

He shook his head. "She still has a thing for him just as I thought. Did she want us to do anything?"

"No. At this point there's nothing we can do. She said Deborah, Lawrence's wife, had called her and said he thought his lawyer could bail him out. He didn't want her to come down to the jail."

"Did she know who the lawyer was?"

"No."

Ty shrugged. "Sounds like all we can do is a little hand-holding."

I WANTED TO stay up for the late news, but my body is programmed to conk out around ten pm so I couldn't make it. But the next morning Channel 6 showed Lawrence Rinehart being led out of the jailhouse by none other than my niece's husband, Cliff Holcomb. Cliff is a successful defense attorney, and I had turned to him for help when Ralph Duncan was killed. Unfortunately he felt the best defense for Ralph's wife Phyllis was to plead insanity which would have placed her in a mental institution for God knows how long, while Ty and I were convinced she didn't do it. The fact that we proved Phyllis was innocent probably did not go down well with Cliff although he's too much of a gentleman to say so. But I'm sure it was embarrassing that a couple of old farts in their seventies solved the case. It wasn't one of his most shining moments.

That afternoon Leah called me again.

"I just heard from Deborah. Lawrence went back to the office so she felt she could speak freely to me."

"Isn't it kind of strange that she would turn to you, his ex-wife, to discuss this?" I suppose I was out of line to ask, but I was very curious about the relationship between these two women.

"Lawrence developed some pretty serious health problems after we divorced. Deborah doesn't have any family around here, and by this point I'd done a lot of soul searching as I told you before, and had established an amicable if not exactly chummy relationship with her. I knew she hadn't seduced him, that he had been the one to initiate their relationship. But when he got sick, she turned to me because she didn't know who else to talk to. He was keeping his health problems a secret from his employees so she couldn't talk to anyone at work, and she was feeling kind of desperate. Our friendship, such at it is, is based on our mutual concern for Lawrence."

"May I ask what those health problems are? It could have some bearing on this case."

"He has early signs of Parkinson's, and the doctors have confirmed that he has it. There are little things Deborah and I notice, but it's not bad enough yet that other people are aware of it."

"How old is Lawrence?"

"A little younger than me. He's sixty-eight."

"So why doesn't he just retire?" I asked. I worked into my early seventies, but luckily I didn't have any health problems.

"His agency is his life. He says he'd be miserable if he retired. But the board of directors is a tough bunch and would probably force him out if they knew about his health. That's why he's so hush-hush about it."

"But one of these days his symptoms are going to get worse. Then he won't be able to hide it any more."

"He says he'll deal with it when it gets to that point. But he'll do everything he can to put it off as long as possible."

"I see," I said, though I wasn't sure I really did. But I know a lot of men simply implode when they can no longer work. They seem to lose the essential part of themselves. It's sad when they don't realize they can reinvent themselves and find new meaning in life by becoming involved in other things. That's what I love about GH. You can't be bored when there are lectures, concerts, parties, discussions, and classes to attend right downstairs.

"So, anyway, you started to tell me that Deborah called. What did she have to say?"

"Lawrence was arrested because they narrowed down the time of death to between about six pm Friday night and two am Saturday morning. And he couldn't establish an alibi for much of that time."

"What does he say he was doing then?"

"It does sound pretty lame I'll have to admit. But he's always been interested in astronomy, ever since he was a kid. He said a huge meteor shower was scheduled for Friday night. He was very anxious to see it and knew he could get a much better view if he drove some distance out into the countryside away from all the city lights. He asked Deborah if she wanted to go with him, but she had a ticket to go with a girl friend to a play downtown. He wasn't back yet when she got home so she went on to bed. Lawrence claims the meteor shower lasted quite a while and then he fell asleep in the car and didn't wake up until well after midnight. It was close to one when he got in and he didn't wake Deborah."

"Is that all they have on him? That he can't verify where he was?"

"No. Jeremy's wife told the police that he went over to Lawrence's house to confront him and that was the last she ever saw of him. Lawrence claims he must have been gone when Jeremy showed up. And of course Deborah was at the play. But they found traces of his blood on the front porch."

"Why was he going to confront him? I know you said he fired Jeremy but wasn't that a few months ago?"

"He said Lawrence had promised him severance pay, but he never got any. And he also felt Lawrence was bad mouthing him around town and that was why he couldn't get another job."

"So is that all you know for now?"

"It is. I'm calling you because Deborah wants you and Ty to get involved."

"Why for heaven's sake? I don't see what we can do."

"She knows you and I were together when we found Jeremy's body. And she also knows about your connection to Cliff Holcomb from the newspaper articles about the murder of Ralph Duncan. So while Lawrence is confident that Cliff will give him the best defense, she's not so sure since you were the one who managed to exonerate Ralph's wife. I guess she wants you to follow behind Cliff and make sure he's going in the right direction."

"I can't do that. Cliff isn't going to talk to me about the case. Especially now. He's supersensitive over the fact I proved him wrong."

"Then you and Ty investigate it on your own."

"I don't think so, Leah. We're not private investigators."

"But you're as smart as any of them are."

"The Ralph Duncan case was a fluke."

"Please!!!"

"Sorry."

SEVEN

I TOLD TY about Leah's call that night at dinner. "Do you think I was right in turning her down? It's not like it's our job to go around solving murders. Besides, I couldn't afford to embarrass Cliff again. I do want to maintain a good relationship with them. They're my only relatives."

"I agree," he said. "Though I have to admit it was a real rush to exonerate Phyllis. But that was one of our GH family. I don't know Lawrence Rinehart from Santa Claus."

"True."

We dropped the subject and went on to discuss other things.

IT WAS JUST after three on Saturday when Leah called me again.

"This is turning into a disaster!" she cried.

I was getting really irritated with her now. Was she going to keep on bugging me indefinitely? "What happened?"

"They've arrested Deborah as an accessory after the fact. They think she helped Lawrence dispose of the body."

Good god! This was getting stranger and stranger.

"Do you know any details?"

"I talked to Lawrence after they interrogated and booked her. He's waiting for Cliff to get her out now."

"So what did he say?"

"It seems they think Lawrence never left the house. When Jeremy came over he killed him. And when Deborah came home from the theater, she helped him dispose of the body."

"How on earth did they come up with that? That's bizarre."

"From what Cliff found out they discovered Jeremy's blood on a tarp in their garage, and some small stains in the trunk of the car. I guess they felt Lawrence couldn't have carried the body so far into the woods by himself and Deborah helped him. They found her hairs and DNA on the tarp along with Lawrence's and of course Jeremy's."

"Since it was in their garage it seems logical their DNA would be on it."

"Especially since she used it when she did some painting."

"But Jeremy's! That is damning. I don't know what to say, Leah. This is too strange for words."

"I know all this stress is going to take a toll on Lawrence's health. It was bad enough when he was arrested. Now he's overwhelmed with the whole mess. They so desperately need help."

"I'm sure Cliff can handle it."

"He's probably good enough, but he seems to be a very busy man. Lawrence needs some hand-holding at this point. I think it would take a little of the stress away if you could talk to him. Just listen to him and hear what he has to say. Then, if you're still not interested, you can always turn him down."

I knew I was on a very slippery slope here. If I agreed to talk to him I was sure it would be very hard to say I wouldn't help. But Leah sounded so pitiful and I'm such a sucker.

"Let me think about it and talk to Ty. I'll get back to you."

I finished doing the load of wash that the phone call

had interrupted then sat down with a book I was halfway through. But I was feeling very restless. I couldn't get Leah's phone call out of my mind, and I knew I needed to make a decision whether or not to get involved. I felt suddenly claustrophobic. The apartment had been closed up tight for weeks with the air conditioning on high during the heat wave. But I felt the need for fresh air. I opened the door to the balcony and stepped outside.

The first thing I noticed was the chattering of birds. I could tell something had upset them. Then I looked over toward the woods and saw Sweetie emerge from the forest looking thin, her hair matted and dirty. She walked slowly as if exhausted.

"Sweetie!" I screamed. "Don't move!"

She looked up at me and sat down on the grass.

I flew out of the apartment, ran down the stairs to the bottom floor because it was faster than the elevator, and tore out the door of the community room. Thankfully nothing was going on in there at the time or they would have thought I'd lost my mind.

Sweetie was still sitting at the edge of the lawn. and I ran over to her and picked her up. I swore I could feel her bones. I held her close and petted her although her fur was knotted with burrs and twigs. "I'm so glad to see you," I whispered in her ear. She purred contentedly.

I carried her back to the apartment worried she might try to struggle out of my arms, but I think she was too weak and hungry. I filled her bowl to the top with food next to a big bowl of water. Normally I measure it out, but today she could eat all she wanted.

She tore into it and ate so fast I realized I'd probably pay for it with cat upchuck on my white carpet. But I was so happy to see her I'd forgive her anything.

When she was finally sated I sat down with her in my

recliner with a comb and brush and worked at getting all the tangles and burrs out. A few I had to cut out with manicure scissors, but most I could work out gently. She seemed so relieved to be rid of them she didn't try to get away but sat quietly and let me do the job. Every few minutes I had to stop and cuddle her and tell her again how glad I was to see her.

When I met Ty for supper a little later he said, "Well, you look like the Cheshire Cat. What's happened?"

"Sweetie's back," I said.

"Oh, I'm *so* relieved!" he said closing his eyes and putting his hands together as if in prayer. "Do you think she's been wandering in the woods all this time?"

"If you could have seen her fur you'd know for sure. It took me over an hour to get out the tangles and all the little mess that got caught in it. She's thin too. She ate like there's no tomorrow."

"Well, I guess that's a good omen for something."

"I was kind of thinking that too. Let's get a table and I'll tell you about my latest call from Leah."

After we ordered I told him about Deborah's arrest and Leah's plea for our help.

"It just gets worse and worse, doesn't it?" Ty said when I finished.

"I pretty much told her no. But I can't help wonder if Sweetie's return is some sort of a sign."

"A sign? Are you into mumbo jumbo now?"

I waved him off. "Come on. Be serious. Maybe it means we're supposed to help out Lawrence and Deborah."

Ty shook his head. "You want *me* to be serious? Believing in signs and portents is nonsense."

That hurt. "Okay. Forget I mentioned it."

I was mad and I barely spoke to him throughout the meal. He kept trying to get a conversation going, but I just concentrated on my food and muttered "yes" or "no" without looking him in the eye. I didn't linger after dessert the way we usually do, but excused myself and went back upstairs to my apartment leaving him sitting at the table. I knew I was acting childish, but my emotions were on a roller coaster and it was better to be alone while I dealt with them.

When I entered my apartment I was greeted by a big pool of upchuck in the middle of the living room carpet which brought me swiftly back down to earth. I sat down and began laughing so hysterically I finally ended in tears. I was a mess.

As I was on my knees cleaning up after Sweetie, someone knocked on my door. It's too hard to get up once I'm down so I just hollered, "Come in!"

It was Ty. When he saw me on my knees he asked, "Are you praying for my soul, Vi?"

I continued my scrubbing. "No, I'm praying to the cat god to keep Sweetie from throwing up any more. I don't think the stain is going to come out of this carpet. Who ever dreamed up putting white carpet in these apartments anyway?"

"They figured us old folks wouldn't be bringing in dirt. We're just as dirty as everyone else." When he realized how that sounded he laughed. "I've heard of dirty old men but not dirty old women."

"You'd be surprised." I scrubbed some more. "Well, that's the best I can do. Help me up, will you?" I put out my hand and he gave me a pull up.

"Where is the rascal anyway?" he asked.

"Asleep on my bed."

"Well, she's probably worn out so I won't disturb her. But I do want to give her a hug and welcome her back."

"I'll convey your message to her when she wakes up."

"Look, Vi, I came to apologize. I'm sorry I made fun of you at dinner."

I sighed. Ty was too special to stay mad at. I knew I had behaved childishly, but I hate being put down. "Don't belittle me, Ty. I wouldn't do that to you."

"Can we sit down and discuss this?"

I pointed to the couch and I sat in my recliner although it needed a good going-over with a lint roller after I'd combed Sweetie in it. I know that half the time I walk around with cat hair on my slacks.

"Okay now," Ty said. "You said Sweetie's return might be a sign we're supposed to help the Rineharts."

"Are you going to make fun of me again?"

He put one hand in the air and the other on his heart. "Scout's honor. I will not. I want to know your thoughts."

I bit my lip wondering if I was about to take a dive off a steep cliff into shallow water. "I seemed to me that since Sweetie's escape started this whole thing, her return might mean we're supposed to stay involved. I know it doesn't make much sense, but I can't help feeling that way."

He smiled. "I should trust your gut feelings, Vi. They certainly worked before. Who would have thought a dead parrot could lead to a murder suspect? Only you."

"Leah says that Lawrence is desperate to talk to us. That's the least we can do."

"Well, I guess we can do that much. Let's take it one step at a time. If we feel there's nothing we can do are you willing to back off?"

"Of course. I know this will not go over well with Cliff should he find out. So I do want to tread carefully."

"We've got a ready-made motto: 'Don't step in the cat barf.'"

I couldn't help but chuckle. "You always know the right thing to say, Ty."

EIGHT

I CALLED LEAH back and told her we were willing to talk to Lawrence. "Absolutely no promises, however. We're just going to hear him out."

"Oh thank you, thank you. Deborah is back home so you can talk to them both."

"How do we do this?"

"I'll tell them to call you and set up a time."

"By the way, Leah, Sweetie showed up today."

"Oh, Vi, I'm so glad. You'll never know how upset I've been over that. Is she okay?"

"Hungry and covered with burrs and knots in her fur but otherwise unharmed."

"You made my day."

I didn't tell her it was Sweetie's return that prompted me to talk to them.

Within ten minutes I got a call from Deborah. "It's so kind of you to meet with us. Could you come to our house tomorrow?"

"I think we're both free in the afternoon."

"How about two o'clock?"

She gave me directions which I wrote on a pad beside my phone. Ty was still there, so I told him the plan.

"Let's go to Sunday brunch a little early to make sure we get out in time," he said. "How about meeting in the dining room about a quarter to twelve?"

THE RINEHARTS LIVED in the same area as Cliff and Greta, about three blocks away. I prayed that Cliff wouldn't be driving around the neighborhood and see Ty's little red convertible in their driveway. It is rather distinctive looking with a Brown University sticker on the back bumper. Not many people in this area have gone to Brown, an Ivy League school with a rather low profile, or even know much about it. I should have driven my car which sort of fades into the woodwork it is so nondescript. If we ever came back here I would suggest that.

Both Lawrence and Deborah met us at the door. Lawrence was a good looking man, tall and well-built with just a dash of white at his temples, the kind of man department stores like to feature in their ads for high-end suits. His eyes were a startling blue and his nose was Roman, straight and distinctive. He seemed younger than the sixty-eight Leah had said he was. Wearing expensive-looking slacks and a crisp white shirt open at the neck, he had the look of self containment and authority that characterize successful men. It was only when he shook my hand I noticed a slight tremor. I wasn't surprised that he'd been able to conceal his illness from his business staff.

On the other hand, Deborah wasn't what I expected. While Leah was stylish and svelte, Lawrence's second wife was short, plump and dressed in blue jeans and a stretched-out white tee, with her reddish-blond hair pulled back in a limp ponytail. She appeared to be around twenty years younger than Lawrence. But she had a lovely smile, at once welcoming and grateful.

The couple invited us into their living room, which was comfortable but unpretentious. Deborah obviously didn't have Leah's talent for decorating, but the well-used furniture looked inviting, the kind you can flop onto without worrying if you're dirtying it or moving a throw pillow out of place. There were books stacked all around, on tables, a hassock and even a small pile on the hearth. A large black and white cat sat atop a pile of magazines on an end table.

"What's your cat's name?" I asked after we all sat down.

"Oreo," she said. "You know. Black and white. Dumb isn't it?"

"It happens to be my favorite cookie. You can blame it on me." Lawrence looked at her tenderly. Their demeanor revealed considerable affection between them.

They seemed pretty relaxed considering the predicament they were in. Leah had told me earlier that Deborah was hysterical. I wondered if they were putting on a front, or if they were now convinced they would triumph because of their innocence. Unfortunately guiltless people don't always get off. The Innocence Project has proven that.

"Can I get you something to drink?" Deborah asked. "Iced tea? Cold drink? Coffee? All are made and ready to go."

Ty asked for coffee, but I try not to drink it after noon so I asked for tea. I knew in the South it comes already sweetened unless you specify otherwise. But I was happy with the sweet.

She brought drinks for everyone including tea for Lawrence and herself then settled in beside her husband.

"So tell us what's going on," I said. "Leah has probably overstated our ability to work things out satisfactorily. The last case was something of a fluke I'm afraid. I can't promise we'll get involved, and if we should, I can't promise a good outcome."

Ty piped up. "You understand that we have absolutely no training in criminal defense or even investigation. We helped Phyllis Duncan because she was a neighbor and because we were convinced she wasn't guilty."

Lawrence sat up straight. "Nor are we. These charges are ridiculous."

Deborah's smile had gone. "I can't believe this is happening to us."

"Cliff Holcomb is a very good defense lawyer, you know," I said. "It puts me in an uncomfortable position to be talking to you at all. Do you know he's my niece's husband?"

"Leah told us," Deborah said. "I was hoping we could do this so no one is aware of your involvement."

"We respect Cliff," Lawrence added. "We also know he is working on a couple of other pretty high profile cases. We're just a little concerned we could get short shrift."

"No you won't," I said. "I know Cliff better than that." I hoped I was right about that but I had no way of being sure.

"All the same, we'd feel so much better if you could at least spend a little time helping us out. Let me ask you this: what is your favorite thing at Glendon Hills? What activity or group is most valuable to the people who live there?"

What a strange question I thought. There are a lot of special things about GH. Finally I said, "The library. It's all volunteer-run and is filled with donated books. Most of them pretty old. But it probably serves the most people."

"If you would help us, at least for a little while, I'm willing to make a ten thousand dollar donation to your library. You can buy all the books you want."

I was stunned. Our library occasionally gets a small donation of a hundred dollars or so, but we'd so love to be able to buy new books as they are released. How could I turn down such a generous offer? I looked at Ty. "What do you think?"

He rubbed his finger across his lips in thought. "Sheer bribery."

Lawrence laughed. "Are you above taking such a bribe?"

Ty grinned. "I guess not, now that you ask."

"As I said before. I want to make sure that this doesn't get back to Cliff. I'm a little bit on shaky ground with him anyway," I said. "I don't want to cause a rift. They're my only relatives."

"Nobody will hear it from us," Deborah said.

"Okay, then. We've heard your story about what you were doing that night from Leah. Now we need to hear it from you. Let's start with six pm on that Friday. They said the murder happened between six Friday and 2 am Saturday. Tell us everything you did, Lawrence." Oreo jumped up on my lap at that point as if he wanted to make a statement. His purr was loud as I petted him. Another cat omen?

Lawrence and Deborah were sitting side-by-side on the sofa. He took her hand as he began to recount his movements that evening.

"We had dinner around six as always. I'd seen on the early news that there was supposed to be a spectacular meteor shower that evening. Astronomy is my passion, and I was very excited about seeing it. Deborah told me she had tickets with her girlfriend, Eliza, to go see 'Ain't Misbehavin'' at the Piedmont Stage that night. She'd told me about it earlier and I'd begged off. Musicals aren't my thing. But I'd forgotten it was that night. So as soon as dinner was over, I told her I was going to drive out of the city where there were no lights so I could see the meteor shower better."

"What time was that?"

"Oh, around seven-fifteen I think."

"But it doesn't get dark till much later. Why leave then?" Ty asked.

Good thinking, Ty.

"I had some work to catch up on at the office. So I went there first."

"Anyone else there who could verify that?" I asked.

"No. You know how Fridays are. Everyone wants to

leave early. I think half the staff was on their way to the beach."

"Did you use the phone?" asked Ty. "A phone record could establish you were there."

"No I didn't. Besides it wouldn't account for the rest of the evening."

"So when did you leave the office?" I was wondering if anyone saw his car in the parking lot and if it would do any good if they had.

"Around nine I guess. I was mainly waiting till it got dark. Then I drove out of town about twenty miles. Far enough away so no city lights would interfere with seeing the meteors."

"What road did you take?" asked Ty.

"Poplar Church Road. It's the least populated, darkest road I could think of in this area."

"That's unfortunate. That means there's less chance anyone saw you."

Lawrence gave a wry smile. "I wasn't thinking about having to establish an alibi. That was the furthest thing from my mind."

"Do you remember exactly where you stopped to watch the sky?" I asked.

"Not sure. Just remember pulling off onto a dirt road. I didn't think anyone would be going that way, and since Poplar Church is narrow with woods on both sides, there aren't a lot of places to stop. I drove down the dirt road a little way till I came to a field with an open sky."

"Do you think you could find that turn-off again?"

"Gosh, I'm not sure. Everything looks so different in the daylight. But I guess I could try. Why?"

"Just trying to cover all the bases. You never know when some little detail can help."

"Leah said you didn't get home until around one," Ty said. "Why so late?"

"I watched the shower for an hour or so. Then I realized how sleepy I was. I'd had a very stressful week with late nights. I was a little afraid to drive home feeling so tired, so I took a nap. Woke up around twelve-thirty or so and drove home."

I turned to Deborah. "Weren't you worried about him when he was out so late?"

"Not really. He's so into stargazing. It's not that uncommon for him to drive out of town just to watch the stars, and he can be gone for hours. When he starts talking about Scorpius and Hercules, the Double-Double and the Coat Hanger he loses me. It's not my thing, so I don't go with him."

"So, what time did you leave for the theater, Deborah?" Ty asked.

"Around seven-twenty-five. The play started at eight and it takes a little while to drive downtown and park."

"And you got home when?" I asked.

She stopped to think a minute. "It was around ten-thirty. I wanted to watch the early Fox news but it was half over."

"So if something happened here at your house it happened between seven-twenty-five and ten-thirty," I said.

"Unless it happened after I fell asleep around eleven-fifteen and before Lawrence returned home."

"I'm sure the police have talked to the neighbors. Did anyone see anything?" I asked.

"Apparently not," Lawrence said. "Our lots are all large and there's so much shrubbery and trees intruders can skulk around without anyone noticing. That's why we've had a rash of burglaries in this neighborhood that the cops can't seem to stop."

"Did either of you notice the blood on your porch when you came home that night?"

"No," Deborah said. "Since it was at the other end of the porch from the front door I never saw it. Besides, it wasn't that much blood. It looked like a small rusty stain that could have been made by dead leaves. Even if I'd seen it, I wouldn't have realized what it was."

"Same with me," Lawrence added.

"What about the tarp?" Ty piped up. We'd developed a team approach to questioning, alternating back and forth. What I didn't think to ask, he always did and vice versa.

Lawrence closed his eyes and held his outstretched hands palm up in supplication. "That's what I really don't get. How could Jeremy's blood get on our tarp? It's a dirty old thing that Deborah used a couple of years ago when she repainted the bathroom. I helped her spread it out on the floor so of course it has my DNA too. And even worse, they found some blood in the trunk of my car. My car was gone until one that night. It's insane."

"Is your garage locked at all times?"

Lawrence thought about it for a minute. "Well, of course the garage door is operated either from a remote or a switch inside the garage. But, come to think of it, I did open a window at the rear of the garage to let in a little air. It can get unbearably hot in there in the summer."

"Aren't you concerned intruders can get into your house that way since it's attached?" I asked.

"No, we have an alarm on the door that goes into the house, so I didn't worry about it. It's as secure as any of the other doors. There's nothing of value in the garage except the cars and we always keep them locked."

"I hate to say this," Ty said, "but the cops have got a lot

of convincing evidence. Do either of you have any idea how all this happened?"

Deborah looked at Lawrence and they both shrugged. "Haven't a clue," they said in unison.

NINE

"I GUESS WE need to know more about your relationship with Jeremy," I said. "I understand you two had been friends for a long time."

Lawrence massaged his forehead with his fingertips for a couple of minutes as if a headache was coming on "We were fraternity brothers at the University," he finally said. "He always was kind of a wild guy, loved to party. That's when his drinking began. I liked the guy a lot, at least then. We talked about going into business together when we graduated, but I soon realized he had a real problem with his drinking and decided I'd be in a world of trouble to count on him. So we each went our separate ways, but always kept in touch."

"Did he go with the TV station right out of school?" Ty asked.

Lawrence nodded. "He did. He started out in some lowly position—I forget just what—and worked his way up to anchor. He had one of those outgoing personalities that just drew people in. He seemed perfect for the job. I saw him occasionally but not often. Leah, who was my wife then, didn't like him much. I assumed he'd conquered his need for drink, but apparently I was wrong."

"But you hired him when he got out of jail for driving drunk and hitting that woman. Why was that?" I asked.

Lawrence picked up Deborah's hand and patted it. He looked at her as he said, "One of the dumbest things I've ever done. I felt sorry for him, and that outweighed common sense I guess."

Deborah squeezed his hand in support. "No good deed goes unpunished as they say. Lawrence is soft hearted. Nobody would hire Jeremy after what he'd done, and Lawrence felt some kind of loyalty to him since they'd been friends for so long."

"Yeah," Lawrence said. "Then the bastard goes and not only hits on Deborah, but steals from me. Of course he denied it. Then he had the audacity to claim I owed him severance pay. I knew he had personal problems but I hadn't dreamed he'd turned into such a total jerk."

"Deborah?" I looked at her wanting to get her input.

"I guess he couldn't help himself when he hit on me. He thought of himself as God's gift to women, and from what I understand, he came on to most of the females in the office. I found him pretty repulsive."

"So Leah was right all along in her assessment of him," Ty said.

"Yes, if I had known how she felt about him, I would have tried to persuade Lawrence not to hire him."

Lawrence looked a little sheepish. "I guess women's antennas are more highly attuned to that sort of thing than ours are. I just thought Leah was overacting."

"You gotta wonder what his wife thought about him. Seems to me she had reasons to want to get rid of him," Ty said.

"I don't know," Lawrence shrugged. "She stood by him while he was in prison. If ever she had a reason to leave him it was then."

I decided to change the subject. "What do you know about the woman he hit? I understand she's confined to a wheelchair. Does she have a husband or relative who might want revenge for that?"

"She does have a husband. I don't know much about either of them. But the accident happened about three years ago. Do you think he'd wait this long for revenge?"

Now it was my turn to shrug. "Things might have happened like they ran out of hospitalization or she got worse or something. Who knows what motivates people."

"Do you think we've given you enough to look into it?" Lawrence asked.

It was sounding pretty impossible to me but I wasn't going to say so out loud. "We'll see what we can do," I said, "but please don't have any expectations about what we can accomplish. I guess for a start you could give us the names and addresses of the people who work for you and your nearest neighbors."

"Got a computer?" Lawrence asked. "I'll email the information."

"That would be great," Ty said. He's far more computer literate than I am though I have a very old one I use on occasion for email. He pulled out his wallet and handed Lawrence his business card. As far as I knew it was only the second time he'd ever used one of them. It said "Tyrone Landowski, retiree extraordinaire" and gave his phone and email address.

On the way back to Glendon Hills Ty and I had little to say to each other. I think we were trying to absorb all the information that Lawrence and Deborah had told us and process it. Frankly as far as I was concerned it sounded like a slam dunk for the prosecutor. But Leah was convinced they were innocent, and they sure hadn't come across as killers to me.

Finally I said to Ty, "I don't even know where to start. Got any ideas?"

"Why don't we talk to Jeremy's wife? I'm sure she has a lot to say."

"What makes you think she'd even talk to us? I'll bet anything the prosecutor has told her not to discuss the case with anyone outside of the cops or his office."

"Yeah. I'm sure you're right. But here's a thought. Maybe I can do some research and find a relative like a sister or brother. Maybe they could tell us something."

"You're a sly one, Ty," I said. "I'm game. See what you can come up with." I had faith in him coming up with information because he uses the internet like it's a magic wand. I'm always amazed at what he can find on it.

MONDAY MORNING WHEN we had our usual coffee in the café before exercise class Ty told me he had found a sister to Amy Scofield.

"Her name is Suzi Wallace and she lives in High Point. Amy has other siblings but they don't live nearby." High Point is the nearest town to Guilford City, "the Furniture Capital of the World" as they call themselves, though most of the furniture industry has long ago moved to China. The reason they can keep the title is the fact that twice a year they hold an International Furniture Show which draws in 80,000 sales people from all over the world. That's close to the entire population of High Point.

"So how do we approach her?" I asked. "We can't tell her we're working to help Lawrence."

Ty thought about it as he sipped his coffee.

"You could tell her you do freelance feature articles for that free newspaper they put out around town? What's its name?"

"Oh you mean the *Guilford Gossip*. The one that likes to dig up dirt. You think she'd talk to someone from that rag?" I asked. "Besides, what do you mean by *you*. I don't want to do this without you."

"It would be suspicious for two of us to claim we're

writing a column together. She'd probably believe you sooner than she would me, and she might want to get some things off her chest. I'm sure she thinks Lawrence is guilty, but who knows what kind of information she might have?"

"What if the cops have told her not to talk?"

"I highly doubt that. She's too removed from the case. But I'm sure she knows what's on her sister's mind. And she might think talking to you will help nail Lawrence."

I was doubtful, but I agreed to call her and see if we could set up an appointment.

AFTER LUNCH I called her though I had many misgivings. I hadn't gotten used to misrepresenting myself, but I kept telling myself it was all for the cause of justice. To my surprise she didn't hesitate. "I'd love to talk to you," she said. "Where do you want to meet?"

"How about Austin's?" Austin's was a restaurant on Main Street in High Point that had been there for years. We agreed to meet at three o'clock. She'd told me she'd be wearing white capris and a navy T-shirt and that she was blond. I spotted her immediately. Of course there were few people in the restaurant at that hour, but she would have stood out in any crowd. To describe herself as a blond was an understatement. She was the kind of blond who turns heads and the tight fitting clothes that clung to her shapely body had a lot to do with it too. Suzi Wallace was a knockout.

She seemed surprised when I sat down opposite her. "Are you Vi?" she asked.

"I am."

She stuttered a little. "I just didn't expect…uh…someone like you…uh…to be writing for that newspaper."

I'm sure my age threw her. I smiled. "My dear, *The Guilford Gossip* searches for the truth even though the truth might be uncomfortable." I hoped I didn't look as nauseated as I felt defending the rag. "Now, can I buy you an iced tea or cup of coffee?"

"Tea would be good, unsweetened of course," she said, brushing back the long hair that kept falling over her right eye. This was a gesture that happened often during our chat. I kept wondering why she didn't secure it with a head band or barrette or something. I guess it seemed sexier that way. It would have driven me crazy.

I ordered iced tea for us both, though I took mine sweet, and when our drinks were served I said, "I'm a little surprised you agreed to talk to me."

"Why?" She pushed back her hair again.

"Well, with Lawrence and Deborah Rinehart indicted for the death of your brother-in-law, I would think you'd let justice take its course and keep a low profile. Or do you think if you speak out you can garner more support towards getting a guilty verdict?"

"Hell, no!" she said angrily.

"Excuse me?" I was shocked at her response.

"I want just the opposite. My brother-in-law was a sleazeball, and I doubt very much the Rineharts are responsible for his death. Lawrence tried to help him out when he got out of jail, for god's sake, and how did Jeremy repay him? By siphoning off money from the business and putting the moves on his wife."

I wasn't sure how she knew all this, but she probably heard it through Amy. "And you don't think that was motive enough for Lawrence to kill him?"

"My ex-husband and I used to get together on occasion with my sister and Jeremy and the Rineharts. This was before Jeremy screwed up and went to jail. But Lawrence was always the gentleman. I just can't believe he did anything like that" She hesitated. "Wait a minute. Aren't you going to take notes or tape me or anything?"

I had put a small notebook in my purse on which to take notes, but I was so unused to impersonating someone other than who I really was, I'd forgotten all about it. I felt like a fool.

I delved into my purse and pulled out the notebook. "I just like to warm up my subjects," I said, "before I start writing anything down. I guess we're ready now." I wondered when she was going to call me out for the fake I was.

"I want you to write about the real Jeremy Scofield. I'll never know what my sister saw in him, and she'd no doubt hate me for doing this, but I can't see an innocent man go to jail. Come to think about it I don't want you to print my name. Just say your source is anonymous."

"Okay, so tell me more about him."

"He thought that women swooned over him, I guess because he was a TV anchor. I'll tell you something off the record if you promise not to write about it."

I turned my pad over and laid down my pen. "Sure." I was grateful for anything she wanted to tell me.

"My husband and I went with Jeremy and Amy to a Christmas party given by the TV station at a downtown hotel. Everyone was drunk as a skunk including myself. I was so wasted that Jeremy managed to get me off in a side room and he put the moves on me. I was too far gone to resist. Well, my husband caught us in the act and that was the end of our marriage. Of course I wasn't entirely innocent, but Jeremy had been foisting drinks on me all evening. I think he'd planned it all along, but I was too stupid and too drunk to realize what he was doing."

I tried not to look shocked but acted as if this was a common everyday event. "So what did Amy think about all this?"

"Amy doesn't know to this day. I'm sure she knows about his other affairs, but it would have devastated her to know he was doing it with her own sister. I love her too much, and this would destroy our relationship."

"But it killed your marriage."

"We were having some difficulty anyway. I think we might have worked it out, but this put the nail in the coffin. Roger couldn't forgive me that." She looked down at her hands folded in her lap, her hair falling over her face as if she didn't want me to see her expression. She seemed genuinely sad.

I gave her a minute to collect herself. Finally I asked, "So you say Amy knew about his other affairs. But she still stayed with him?"

"She was in denial. She fell head over heels for the schmuck years ago, and she's been making excuses for him ever since. It was always the woman's fault: whoever he was doing it with led him on. Even when he hit that woman she had an excuse for him. The woman shouldn't have been walking in the road with dark clothing at night. You can quote me on this part, though I still want you to say your source is anonymous."

I wasn't sure any reputable paper would use such a source, but then the *Guilford Gossip* wasn't what I considered reputable. Besides, I had to remind myself, I wasn't actually writing any article. "Okay," I said and turned over the pad and scribbled something down. "So I understand Amy says Jeremy went to the Rinehart's house that night to confront Lawrence over severance pay. Why should he get severance pay if he was fired for taking money from the firm?"

Suzi pushed her hair back again. I wanted to offer to buy her a headband but I restrained myself. "That's probably another of Jeremy's lies, or else Amy made that up as an excuse for him going out that night. He probably had a rendezvous with some woman."

"I'm going to share something with you, Suzi, that hasn't yet been made public. But the police have found evidence at the Rinehart's house that implicates both Lawrence and Deborah. It's pretty damning stuff."

Her mouth fell open in shock. "What kind of evidence?"

"Well, I suppose it will come out sooner or later. There were some blood stains on the porch and in the trunk of his car."

"You gotta be kidding!" She was so startled she forgot to push back her hair and it slipped over her eye making her look like a waif.

"No I'm not. So what are your thoughts on that?"

She didn't hesitate a minute. "Someone set him up. There's no other answer. I simply can't believe Lawrence Rinehart is guilty of murder."

"What about Deborah?"

"I haven't seen him since he married Deborah. My marriage broke up and Jeremy went to jail so we haven't gotten together. But I can't believe they did it. This is absurd."

That was my theory too. I was glad to hear she agreed with me. "In that case, can you think of anyone who might want to do that?"

She pulled back her hair and twisted it into a roll at the back of her neck as she thought. "Not at all. I can't think of a soul who would want to harm him. Granted I know nothing of the relationships at his office. Nor do I know who he and Deborah socialize with. But still…"

I'd been pretend writing all this time. Suzi was giving me an interesting take on this whole thing but it wasn't what I expected. I thought she would be defending her sister's husband. What she told me just made me feel more confident that the Rineharts were innocent, but I hadn't gained any information that would help their case.

I thanked her for talking to me and got up to leave.

"Do you know when the article will be in *The Gossip*?" she asked.

I shrugged. "You never know what the editor will like and what he won't. Since I'm freelance I can never count on anything. But, hopefully, soon."

The poor girl would be unsuccessfully searching the *Guilford Gossip* for a long time to come.

TEN

I CALLED TY when I got home and shared our conversation with him.

"That's the opposite of what I thought she'd say. He must have been a real creep. But did you learn anything that might help Lawrence?" he asked.

"Only her opinion that he couldn't have done it. She'd be a good character witness for him should it come to trial."

"Let's hope it never gets that far. But unfortunately there's too much damning evidence. That's what we've got to work on."

"I'm sure you're right. But how?"

"I haven't a clue. Let's think about it and discuss it over dinner."

Deborah called me shortly after I hung up.

"Hey, Vi. I thought of something for you."

"What's that?"

"Jeremy wasn't the only employee Lawrence had to fire. He let someone go just two or three weeks ago."

"Who was that?"

"Her name was Rosalind Voncannon."

"Why'd he fire her?"

"She was a slacker. She spent more time flirting with the guys than doing her work. He gave her several chances to improve, but her work didn't get any better so he let her go."

"D'you think she wanted to get back at him?"

"She put on a pretty good scene the day she left. She never said she'd get him back, but she was damn mad."

"We should talk to her then. Do you know how she can be reached?"

"I can give you the address where she lived when she was at the firm. Don't know if she's still there."

She gave me a phone number as well, and I tried it right away only to find it was no longer in service. I called Ty and asked if he wanted to drive by the townhouse where she lived so see if she was there. It wasn't far from GH, only about three miles, but when we drove by the property there was a "For Rent" sign in the front yard and we could tell the interior was empty.

It was time for Ty to use his computer research skills. He said he'd see what he could find before we met for dinner. This gave me a chance to go to the pool and swim laps which I hadn't done for a while. I participate in the Masters program and have won medals in swimming competitions in my age group. I usually swim pretty regularly but I hadn't had time recently except for one water aerobics class. We have a beautiful pool and hot tub/spa at GH, and it's a wonderful perk to be able to go downstairs at any time to use it. I told myself I was going to have to make sure I swam more often.

Ty didn't have to say a word when I met him at 5:30 in the lobby. He simply shrugged his shoulders and held out his hands palm up signaling he came up empty.

That evening after dinner I called Deborah and told her we hadn't been able to locate Rosalind.

"Phone service has been stopped and we drove by the address you gave me. There was a 'for rent' sign in the yard and it was empty. Was she close to anyone at work who might know where she is?"

"Ummm…I'm trying to think. I know she went out

to lunch with several of her coworkers. I'm not sure they were close friends, but I could give you a couple of those names. They might know something."

"Can't hurt to try."

"Just so you'll know…I doubt she's smart enough to set up a scheme to blame this on Lawrence. Somebody had to be pretty clever to plant that evidence."

"Sometimes women play dumb because they think it will attract men. She might be a lot more cunning than you think."

"I guess that's possible," she admitted.

I wrote down two names and phone numbers she gave me.

The first one I called went to the answering machine, and I didn't want to leave a message. I got through on the second call.

"Is this Missy Fenstermacher?" I asked.

"That's me. Who's this?"

"My name is Vi Weatherspoon. Deborah Rinehart gave me your name." I hoped that might smooth the way for me since Lawrence was her boss.

"Oh, gosh, how is Deborah? I was so upset when I heard the news about her and Lawrence. It's beyond belief. And the office is in turmoil right now."

"Would it be possible to get together with you to talk about the situation?"

"If it's okay with Deborah it's certainly okay by me. When do you want to do it?"

"The sooner the better. Could I meet you on your lunch break tomorrow? Or I should say we. My friend Ty Landowski will be coming with me."

"Of course. How about the Colonial Tavern? It's close to work."

"Fine. Would 11:45 be okay? I try to get in ahead of the lunchtime rush."

"Perfect. See you then."

I called Ty and told him my plans. "I hope that works for you."

"It'll give us time to shower and dress in street clothes after exercise class."

We try to go to exercise class three times a week although it doesn't always work out that way when we get busy. I really notice it if I miss a session or two. These old bones get creaky if I don't work out like I should.

MISSY TURNED OUT to be older than I expected. I think her name misled me. She appeared to be in her late forties, had a pleasant if unremarkable face, and wore her auburn hair long and straight. Her figure was stocky but she was nicely dressed in a skirt and tailored blouse, pretty unusual in these days of casual attire. I assumed the agency had a dress code since they would meet with clients.

We introduced ourselves and joined her in a booth.

She seemed surprised that two elderly people were questioning her about a murder but apparently was too polite to ask.

"In case you're wondering," I said, "I know Lawrence's first wife, and she asked us to do what we could for Lawrence." I didn't mention that I'd only just met her.

"Oh yes, Leah. I've worked there quite a while and have known both of Lawrence's wives. I've got to say Leah's pretty amazing to be so forgiving. I'm not sure I would have been. But you know they're both nice women. It's a strange world we're living in."

Remembering that Leah had told me no one at the office knew about Lawrence's health problems, I wasn't surprised Missy wondered why Leah still cared about her ex-husband.

"We're here to ask if you know anything about Rosalind Voncannon," Ty said. "We understand she made quite a scene when she was fired. We've not been able to locate her."

Before she had a chance to reply a waitress interrupted us and took our orders. The Colonial Tavern specializes in old-time comfort food so I ordered country fried steak, mashed potatoes and black-eyed peas. I'd never had black-eyed peas till I moved to North Carolina but I've learned to love them and order them whenever possible. Both Ty and Missy ordered Chef salads. I was determined not to feel guilty about it, but it took some effort.

When she left with our orders Missy shook her head and said, "It was embarrassing. Normally our office is very circumspect and business-like. When she threw her hissy fit we were all shocked. None of us was terribly fond of her, but we never expected her to act like that."

"Why did you dislike her so much?" I asked.

"She did as little work as possible. She was far more interested in coming on to the guys, especially Jeremy after he was hired. I couldn't believe her gall."

"We tried her phone number that Deborah gave us but the service has been discontinued. Do you have any idea where she is?"

"I heard via the grapevine she left town."

"Can you be more specific?" Ty asked.

"Not really. She talked about relatives out west, but I don't know if that's where she went."

"Do you have any idea where out west?"

"No. I don't know if she was deliberately vague about it or not."

The waitress brought us our meals and we temporarily suspended questioning Missy while we ate. Finally I asked her, "Tell me what it was like when Jeremy worked at your office."

Missy paused, fork in the air, and rolled her eyes. "Don't know why Lawrence ever hired him. If there ever was anyone stuck on himself it was Jeremy. Even his time in jail didn't seem to make a dent in his self-regard. What a loser."

"You knew that they'd been friends for many years didn't you?" asked Ty. "Lawrence felt some loyalty toward him."

"Yeah, we all knew that. They were so different it's hard to believe they were close. But I guess it's hard sometimes to give up the friendships you made when you were young. We just wished he could have helped him out some other way. Jeremy kept things stirred up all the time." With that she stirred her iced tea vigorously.

"Stirred up how?" I asked.

"Like Rosalind he was hitting on everyone—even me," and she gave a deprecating laugh as if that was unheard of. "And he spent a lot of time bragging about his time at the TV station. He thought he was some kind of big celebrity. He was in a way, only it was because he hurt that woman while driving drunk."

"So if both he and Rosalind were on the hunt, so to speak, why didn't they hook up?" I asked.

Missy shrugged. "Don't know. Maybe they did. But they didn't make it obvious at the office. Why would they keep it secret? I mean everyone knew he wasn't faithful to his wife, so that wouldn't have been a reason."

"Do you have any idea who might know if they were having an affair?" Ty had almost finished his salad while Missy and I had barely begun eating our meals. I dove in trying to catch up while Missy ruminated on his question for a while.

"Candice Knowlton might know. She was tighter with Rosalind than the rest of us," she finally said.

That was the name Deborah had given me along with Missy's.

"Do you think she might know how to get in touch with Rosalind?" Ty asked.

"Could be," Missy said. "You want me to ask her when I go back to work?"

"Do you have a good relationship with her?" I wanted to approach Candice carefully because she might be the last good chance we had of finding Rosalind. I didn't want to scare her off.

She gave a quirky smile. "Not especially. We do go to lunch sometimes, but since all this has happened she's kind of standoffish. Not sure why. But she goes back a way. She and Leah worked pretty closely together and seemed on good terms."

"Then maybe we should do it. Deborah gave me her number. I'll try her tonight."

On the way home from the restaurant Ty and I talked about our conversation with Missy.

"Sounds like there's a lot of drama in that office," Ty said.

"You name me one office where that doesn't happen," I said. "Even at the Girl Scouts where it was all women, there was plenty of drama to go around. Just a different kind. You get a bunch of people in close quarters eight or nine hours a day, there's going to be a lot of undercurrents and personality conflicts. It's all part of the game."

"Tell me about it, Remember I worked for the State Department."

ELEVEN

WHEN WE GOT back to GH Ty challenged me to a game of ping-pong. He's an excellent player and has won tournaments so he's a formidable opponent. I've beat him only a very few times, but that doesn't mean I'm not eager to try. I'm as competitive as he is so it always gets a little heated. That day I won one out of four which isn't too bad considering his prowess. I've invited him to challenge me in a swimming competition, but he always declines. "I don't look good in a swimsuit," he tells me with a grin. He says that because I've griped so often about the women at GH who won't go to water aerobics because they don't like the way they look in a suit, as if any of us in our seventies, eighties and nineties are bathing beauties. Who cares anyway? I guess Ty just doesn't want to get beat.

When I got back upstairs to my apartment I found a voice mail on my phone from my niece Greta. "Auntie, Cliff has had an apparent heart attack. They've taken him to Piedmont Hospital where they're checking him out." The voice mail was sent at 11:35 when we were on our way to the restaurant to meet Missy. It was now 2:15.

I called Ty and told him what had happened and that I was leaving to go to the hospital to be with Greta.

"I'd like to come along, if that's okay," he said. He'd been to their house many times for dinner and was as fond of them as I was.

"Of course. You want me to drive?" I knew that was a foolish question because Ty always prefers to go in his convertible, and he never lets me drive. Frankly I think he's a bit of a sexist when it comes to women driving. He wants to be in control. He says it's because his car has a stick shift, and I have to remind him that I learned to drive in a car without an automatic transmission and owned several more after that.

It took us about twenty minutes to get to the hospital and we found Greta in the emergency room waiting room.

I rushed up to her and gave her a hug. "What's the news?"

"He's upstairs having a catheterization to determine what happened. If they find a blockage they'll decide on whether to use a stent or do surgery. I sure hope they don't decide to operate."

We sat around for the next couple of hours with little conversation, all of us deep into our own private thoughts. I was feeling guilty that we had, in a way, been working behind Cliff's back by talking to the principals in his case. I don't know what the other two were thinking, but I'd guess Greta was wondering if Cliff was going to survive or not.

Finally a doctor dressed in surgical scrubs came into the waiting room. His expression was neutral, showing no sign of the outcome. Greta jumped up and hurried over to him.

"How's my husband?" she asked. I could tell how upset she was from the edge to her voice.

"Looks like he's going to need a triple bypass," the doctor said. "But he's otherwise in good shape. He should do just fine."

She closed her eyes to take this in. She's pretty spiritual so I figured she was saying a silent prayer. I said one with her. "When will this take place?" she asked.

"We'll try to schedule it for tomorrow. You can come see him this evening. Right now we're making sure there's no bleeding where we inserted the catheter."

"Can my aunt and her friend come too?"

"Yes, but don't stay too long. He'll need his rest." With that he left.

Greta turned to us. The color had pretty much drained from her face.

I walked over and put my arms around her. "He'll be fine," I said. "Just fine." Those words sounded so hollow. I knew many people who'd gone through bypass surgery and lived a long and happy life. But there were always those who didn't.

Ty came up and waited till I stepped back and took her hand. "He's a hell of a tough cookie, Greta. You two will be celebrating your sixtieth wedding anniversary some day."

She took her forefingers and wiped away the tears brimming at her eyes. "Well. I've got to get over this weepy stuff. I can't show this face to Cliff." She attempted a weak smile. "Where are you parked? I'll walk out with you."

WE WENT BACK to the hospital at eight that evening and found Greta in Cliff's room. She said she'd gone back home to get a quick bite, pick up something to read and then went to his room as soon as he was assigned one. Cliff was his usual jovial self. He greeted us with, "Haven't you guys got better things to do than visit me in the hospital?" He said it with a smirk and a wink. We're aware that he and Greta have always tried to subtly encourage a romantic relationship between the two of us which neither of us is interested in. We just find it amusing.

"Haven't seen you guys for a while," he said getting serious. "Greta and I had just been talking about having you over for dinner this weekend." It seemed obvious he didn't want to talk about his upcoming surgery. He was putting on a brave face.

"We'll take a rain check. You know how we love Greta's cooking," I said.

"I wanted to have you over because I miss you," he said. "But I also see your name connected to another murder case. How did you manage that?"

My heart turned cold. I didn't want to make a slip of the tongue that would indicate we were any way currently involved in this. Especially not now. He didn't need any extra aggravation. I forced a grin and shrugged my shoulders. "Gosh, Cliff, I seemed to be at the wrong place at the wrong time. Again." I told him that Sweetie jumped off the balcony and ran off into the woods and I had to go look for her.

"Oh, no!" cried Greta. "Did you find her? Is she okay?" Greta loved that cat almost as much as I did.

"I'd about given up hope but she reappeared last Saturday, skinny and covered with burrs and her fur all matted but otherwise okay."

"Oh, thank goodness."

"So you went looking for her in the woods?" Cliff asked. "Why was Leah Rinehart with you?"

I'd forgotten her name was in the paper. "Leah'd come for a tour of Glendon Hills. I volunteer to show people around on weekends when the marketing department is closed. I took her upstairs to show her my apartment, and she was so excited to see the balcony that she ran over and opened the door and Sweetie was out like a shot. She got up on a table, jumped off the railing onto a jut-out on the first floor of building, and then onto the ground. She'd run into the woods by the time I got downstairs. Leah was almost hysterical and insisted on helping me look for her."

"And so that was how you two found Jeremy Scofield's body."

"I'm afraid so."

He gave a low laugh. "Well I'm surprised you haven't wormed your way into the case."

I could feel the heat rise in my face and thanked my stars that I wasn't one to blush. I'd lied already since I'd gotten involved so I wasn't above lying again. The last thing I wanted to do was to get Cliff riled up.

I shrugged. "I know I'm no private investigator. That thing with Phyllis Duncan was a fluke. She was a fellow resident and we're the ones who found her with the knife." I said what I had to say and I didn't have to lie after all. I hoped he accepted that as a denial.

"Look," Cliff said, "I'm not bringing it up because you proved me wrong. I worry about your safety. I think you should stick with activities at Glendon Hills where you're not in danger."

"Oh, Cliff," I said. "Just because I'm seventy-six doesn't mean I don't have good sense."

He looked contrite. "I didn't mean it that way. Of course you do. I just don't think you realize how dangerous the world has become these days."

"Oh for heaven's sake," Greta interrupted. "Can't we talk about something more pleasant?"

"I heard this heat wave is going to be over in a couple of days," Ty said. "I, for one, would welcome that."

And the matter of the Rineharts didn't come up again.

The operation was scheduled for eleven am the next day. Ty and I went to the hospital about ten to be with Greta knowing she'd be frantic. I believe sitting in a hospital waiting room waiting for word about a loved one is just about the most miserable experience you can have. I sometimes think it's easier being the patient because at least you know what's going on. Unless you're unconscious and then you don't care.

We didn't dare all leave to go to the cafeteria at lunch

so Ty went down and carried out some sandwiches and drinks for the three of us. Greta barely picked at her food. My appetite was still pretty healthy and I managed to finish off my meal. I wondered if there'd ever be an occasion when I didn't feel like eating.

It was almost four-thirty when the doctor came out to talk to Greta.

"He did well, and he's still in recovery. He'll be in cardiac ICU for a few days then. Why don't you go home and get some rest, Mrs. Rinehart?"

"No, I'd rather wait here until I can see him."

"It might be several hours yet."

"That's okay. I'll wait."

He finally saw he couldn't persuade her so he left.

Greta turned to us. "You two go home now. I'll be fine now that I know he survived the operation."

"You sure?" I asked.

"Absolutely. I brought a book to read and I think I can concentrate on it now. Shoo, shoo," She made sweeping gestures for us to go.

On the way home I said to Ty, "You know, for some reason, this makes me feel doubly guilty about looking into Lawrence and Deborah's case knowing Cliff is ill."

"Well, don't be. It's probably a good thing we're doing it. The case might get pushed off onto some junior guy who's not as good as Cliff while he's recuperating."

I thought about it for a minute. "I suppose you're right. Do you think he's out of the woods now?"

"Let's hope so."

TWELVE

THAT EVENING I called the number I had for Candice Knowlton. She was my only lead to find Rosalind Voncannon. I hoped she'd be amenable to meeting with us.

A young child answered the phone. "Is your mommy there?" I asked.

She didn't answer but I heard the clunk of the phone as she dropped the receiver and her little voice in the distance hollering, "Mommy, Mommy, some old lady is on the phone for you."

I guess I'm an old grump but I wish people wouldn't allow their kids to answer the phone until they're old enough to know basic courtesy.

After a couple of minutes I heard, "Hello?" I could hear the noise of children playing loudly in the background.

"Is this Candice Knowlton?" I asked.

"Yes." She said tentatively as if fearing what bad news was coming next.

"My name is Vi Weatherspoon and I'm a friend of Leah Rinehart's." That was stretching it a bit but I decided that might be more of an incentive to talk to me than if I'd mentioned Lawrence or Deborah.

"Really? How is she? I miss her."

Well, that was good news and to my advantage. "She's good. But she's awfully upset about what's happening with Lawrence and Deborah, and asked if I could help her."

"Help her? How?"

"Since she's no longer at the office and doesn't feel

comfortable about going there, she asked if I could talk to some of the employees about events that have happened."

"If you're asking about Jeremy's death I don't know a thing."

"But you do know about Rosalind Voncannon, don't you?"

There was silence at the other end. I was afraid she was going to hang up. Finally she said, "What's she got to do with anything?"

"Well I understand she got fired and was pretty bitter about it."

There was another brief silence. "So? She didn't have anything against Jeremy."

"No, but I believe, as does Leah, that someone is trying to frame Lawrence and Deborah."

"I don't think Roz is capable of doing something like that."

"People can surprise you."

"I think I know her better than that. Hold on a minute, will you?" I could tell she held her hand over the receiver because her voice was muted, but I could still hear her yell at her children to "hold it down, will ya?"

"Sorry," she said. "Sometimes the kids get totally out of hand."

"They'll be grown before you know it." I was certainly not the one to make cliché statements like that when I didn't even have any kids. But I was trying to calm her down and make her more amenable to answering my questions. "Have you talked to her lately?"

"She said she was going to take a trip out west to visit some relatives before she came back to job hunt. So, no."

"Did you know her town house is for rent and the phone has been disconnected?"

"What!? Um, no, I didn't." She tried to cover up her shock. "Are you sure about that?"

"Yes, Candice. She seems to be gone. Believe me."

"Why would she do that?"

"You tell me. I understand she put on quite a show when she was fired."

"How would Leah know? She's not there anymore."

"No, but she still knows what happens at the office. And she's wondering if Rosalind might have decided to get back at Lawrence."

"That's insane! Roz would never do anything like that."

"Are you completely sure about that? Why has she disappeared? Why has she left her home unless she's guilty of something?"

Candice sighed. "This is so confusing I don't know what to think. Maybe she moved because she couldn't afford to stay there. Maybe she found a cheaper place."

"Then why did she lie to you about visiting relatives out west?"

"I…I don't know."

"Please help us out if you can. Do you know any of her relatives we could talk to? Any other friends?"

"I know she has a brother. I think he lives in the area, but I can't remember his name."

"It's not Voncannon?"

"No, she was married once. Didn't change her name after she divorced."

"If you remember it, will you call me and let me know?"

A hesitation. "I guess so."

I wasn't sure she really meant it but I gave her my number just in case. This was getting worse and worse. I felt like I was playing Pin the Tail on the Donkey only the donkey was somewhere miles away in the opposite direction. I wondered if Deborah or Lawrence might know Rosalind's brother's name. so I called them after I hung up.

Deborah answered the phone.

"I just learned Rosalind has a brother and he might know her whereabouts. Do you know anything about a brother? His name? Where he might live?"

"Mmmm, gosh, I'm trying to think. All I remember is he worked at an area hospital, though I have no idea which one."

"Is he a doctor?"

"No, no. Some kind of technician, I believe. You know like IV or something like that."

"But you don't know what hospital or remember his name."

"Gosh, I wish I could but I'm drawing a blank."

"Well, thanks anyway. Call me if anything occurs to you."

"Absolutely"

I gave up and went to bed.

Ty AND I met as usual the next morning in the café before our exercise class and I filled him in on my phone calls the night before.

"Looks like we need to go in another direction," he said.

"Great idea. But what? Where?"

"Well…" he thought for a minute. "What if this has nothing to do with someone wanting to get back at Lawrence and Deborah? What if someone just wanted to get rid of Jeremy and found it convenient to pin it on them?"

"Oh!" I said startled. "I hadn't considered that. I was so sure someone was out to get them it hadn't occurred to me they might be collateral damage. So we should find out who had it in for Jeremy. We can't ask his wife so who do we ask?"

"It's been a while since he was at the TV station, but we could start there."

I nodded, "Okay." I looked at my watch. "Uh oh. We better hurry or we'll be late for class. We don't want Spunky to get on our case."

Spunky is our darling fitness instructor and she would never get on anyone's case except to jolly them with smiles and jokes into exercising more. She's convinced that keeping fit is the key to living to a ripe old age, and she does everything she can to encourage our participation in one or more of her many different exercise classes. She urges us on with such enthusiasm it's hard not to join in with equal eagerness. I try to go to Fun and Fit regularly and the water aerobics when I can. And then I do my laps to keep in shape for my Masters competition, so I do pretty well. But I take in as many or more calories than I burn off unfortunately. What can I say?

We decided to visit Cliff at the hospital after lunch. On our way there Ty said, "Remember, now, don't let slip what we're doing for Lawrence and Deborah."

"I know I'm sometimes forgetful," I said trying not to sound irritated, "but I don't think I'm so far gone I'd forget about *that*."

We were both silent the rest of the trip. I only hoped he was feeling remorseful.

Greta was in the waiting room in the ICU unit reading the newspaper, what there was of it in these days of diminished print news.

"So how's the rascal doing?" Ty asked her after we all hugged.

"Very well. Fingers crossed. The doctor says he's progressing nicely."

"Can we see him?" I asked.

She consulted her watch. "There's a fifteen-minute visiting period in about eight minutes. You can see him then."

"I don't want to rob you of your chance to be with him," I said.

"Well, why don't we split it. You stay about eight minutes and I'll go in after you."

Cliff looked pale and as though he'd aged a few years lying there hooked up to multiple monitors while hanging bags dripped liquids through tubes into his veins. Greta had said he was doing well, but you couldn't prove it by me.

"Looks like you could use a whiskey sour," I said referring to his drink of choice. I never know what to say to people when they're ill.

He pointed to the bag of solution hanging over his left shoulder. "What do you think that is? I have a deal with the nurse."

"So what does she get in return?" asked Ty wiggling his eyebrows like Groucho Marx.

Cliff started to laugh but apparently it hurt so he put his hand on his chest over the ridiculous hospital gown with little blue sprigs on it. "She ain't gettin' much till this old ticker heals. Besides Greta won't go home. She's been here day and night. Can't you guys prevail upon her to go home and get some rest?"

"Why?" asked Ty. "So you can engage in some hanky-panky?"

Cliff closed his eyes and shook his head. "You're a dirty old man, Ty. Never suspected."

Ty, realizing he probably overdid it, said, "Seriously, Cliff, is there anything we can do for you?"

"Just like I said. Talk Greta into going home for the night. I'm doing fine. She must be worn-out."

"We'll give it a shot," I said. "But you know her. She can be pretty stubborn."

We talked to Greta when we left his room and told her how concerned he was about her. "I think you'd be doing him a favor if you'd get a good night's sleep tonight," I said. "You don't need to get run-down. You need to be in good shape for when he gets home."

She reluctantly agreed to leave that evening.

THIRTEEN

"I THOUGHT HE looked pretty bad," I said on the way home. "What do you think?"

"Well, I suppose anyone would. That's a rough operation."

"Maybe he'll rebound quickly. I think he's in pretty good shape otherwise. Do you know how long he'll be recovering?"

"I understand it's six to eight weeks before you can go back to your job."

I thought about that for a moment. "Wouldn't it be neat to be able to hand him the solution to this murder as a present by that time?"

"Six to eight weeks? My god I hope it won't take us that long. But, Vi, that might upset him that we solved his case a second time."

That was tricky. I gave it some thought. "We can say we only did it because he was recuperating and we wanted to help him out and take some of the stress off of him."

Ty pulled at his earlobe thoughtfully. "Well, I would hope he'd accept that in the spirit it was given. But knowing him, I'm not really sure."

"Let's take it on faith that he'll be pleased."

He looked at me for a minute then looked back at the road without saying anything more on the way home.

When we got back to GH we played a couple of games of ping pong just to work off our concern over Cliff. Ty won them both. I decided I needed to come up with a challenge in which we were more evenly matched. Neither of us knew chess. He was already an excellent bridge player and I was less than mediocre. I gave it a lot of thought. Suddenly it occurred to me: Scrabble! Maybe I could win a game of that once in a while. I made a mental note to buy a Scrabble game the next time I went shopping.

That night an hour or so after dinner the fire alarm went off. This happens at regular intervals so we don't get too excited about it. The smoke detectors are so sensitive that a piece of burned toast sets it off. The noise is piercing, its decibel reading somewhere off the charts. When I first moved to GH it sounded in the apartments, and all I could do was cower under the covers with my hands clasped over my ears. I guess I was more sensitive to it than many others were, but enough of us complained they fixed it so it only sounds in the hallways and public spaces now. But it's loud enough we can still easily hear it in the apartments as well. And there's a monitor on the living room wall that flashes in case you're deaf. We're told to stay put unless someone tells us otherwise. To this point, no one had ever told us otherwise. I wondered if my new neighbor down the hall had burned his toast again. He'd already set off the alarm twice that brought the firemen to his door.

The siren continued for an unusually long time, and I was beginning to wonder if it was stuck. Then our evening security guy, Tom, knocked at my door.

"Ms. Weatherspoon," he said looking serious, "we're evacuating the apartments just to be safe. Please take the back stairs to the parking lot."

This was so unexpected I couldn't react for a minute. "Good grief," I finally said. "What's going on?"

"There's a fire in the kitchen," he said. "We have three companies here and they are getting it under control. But the fire chief thought it would be wise for everyone to be out of the building."

My place is at the back of the building so I never really know what's going on at the front. I had heard some distant sirens, but the fire department always responds to the alarm so I thought it was a routine call.

Assuming things were as under control as Tom had said, I decided against taking Sweetie with me. I knew I wouldn't be able to hold on to her for any length of time, and she'd probably head for the woods again. I didn't want to take a chance on that.

I usually get into my pajamas and robe after dinner, but this time I got involved paying some bills and hadn't yet gotten out of my clothes. Thank heavens for small favors.

Since it was quite warm outside I didn't need a wrap and decided against taking my purse. I grabbed my keys and headed for the stairs. My neighbors were all coming out of their apartments and joined me in the trek down to the parking lot. There was quite a bit of excited chatter and speculation. I knew I wouldn't see Ty out there because he would be going to the East Wing parking lot on the other side.

Our lot is lower than the main entrance and down a curved drive so a few of us began heading up the drive to see what was going on. A number of fire trucks, pumpers and ladder trucks, several police cars, and an ambulance were parked helter-skelter in front of the main entrance, with blinking and whirling lights pulsating against the darkening sky. It looked like a carnival gone awry. They wouldn't let us anywhere near the action so there wasn't much we could do but stand around and wonder what was happening. Our curiosity quotient was off the charts.

A number of residents on the ground floor where there are patios instead of balconies are dog owners and many of them had their pooches on leashes. They don't usually walk them at the same time, so their pets rarely get to interact. The dogs were having a high old time sniffing each other up and yapping at one another, adding to the surreal atmosphere.

I was standing halfway up the drive watching what little activity I could see when Cora Lee Hillman tapped me on the shoulder.

"Hi, Vi," she said. "What do you think is going on?" She flipped her arm toward the activity up the hill. "I heard the whole first floor is burning."

"I doubt it, Cora Lee. I was told it was in the kitchen and is almost under control."

"My apartment's on the first floor. I hope it doesn't spread there."

"I'm sure it won't," I said trying to sound more positive than I felt. "The fire doors at the end of each corridor should keep it from spreading."

"Well, I'm wondering if this fire was set." Her lips turned up at the corners in a grim smile. Nothing would please her more than having something scandalous going on.

"Why on earth would you think that?" I wanted to roll my eyes but knew she'd be insulted. You do not want to insult Cora Lee.

"You know Arthur Tisdale is always complaining about the food."

"I don't see why. I think the food is just fine. He surely can't be *that* unhappy with it even if he isn't satisfied."

She folded her arms under her ample bosom. "You don't know him very well, do you?"

"No, can't say that I do. Isn't he fairly new?"

"He moved in a couple of months ago. And he's had the kitchen in an uproar ever since. He sends almost all his food back saying it's underdone or overdone or too hot or too cold. There's no pleasing him."

"Somehow I've missed that thank goodness."

"I actually overheard him once saying he might as well burn the kitchen down it was so pitiful. Of course I thought he was kidding at the time." She shrugged her shoulders as if to say don't blame me that I didn't report it to anyone.

"Do you know anything about this guy? What's his background?" If anyone knew the details it would be Cora Lee.

"I heard he ran a restaurant in Cleveland, Ohio. So I guess he thinks he knows all about food. And he hates any Southern food like black-eyed peas, grits, hush puppies and the like. He has a real fit when those were on the menu."

"That's hard to believe!" I exclaimed. "I've fallen in love with all those dishes. It didn't take long to convert me."

"Well, I grew up in the South, and those are manna from heaven." I knew Cora Lee had moved from nearby High Point. Her accent is soft, typical for the area, not like the over-ripe accent of Paula Dean and others from the Deep South. "No, there's something wrong with that man. Just not sure what it is."

I thought she'd finished and I turned around to see what was going on at the top of the hill when she said, "So what's happening with the murdered guy you found out in the woods behind our building? Surely you must be involved again. I don't think you can resist that kind of challenge." It's impossible to dissuade Cora Lee from any topic she wants to latch on to. And it was obvious she had latched on to this one come hell or high water.

She was the last person on earth I would discuss it with. I tried to figure out how I could brush her off without making her mad...or worse, let her know I wasn't telling the truth.

"Nothing's happening that I know," I said, putting on my innocent face. That was true, at least for today.

"Isn't that your niece's husband who's the attorney?" she asked. I knew she would assume I was involved if Cliff represented Lawrence and Deborah.

"Cliff is in the hospital having just had a triple bypass. The case is in limbo for the time being."

"Oh…well, that's too bad. I hope he's doing okay."

"He's doing well thank you."

She lost interest at that point and drifted away.

Since most of us aren't in shape to stand for long periods of time, people began to sit on the grass or on the wall that runs along the back of the parking lot. Residents who live on the first floor brought their folding chairs off their patios and onto the grassy areas to sit on. It was turning into something of a party when some who realized we might be outside for a while brought along bottles of wine and paper cups.

Shortly before midnight, almost four hours after we evacuated, Frank Kaufman, our Operations Manager, came to tell us we could return to our apartments. I'd been sitting on the grass all that time, and John, a neighbor, gave me a hand and pulled me to my feet. It's hell when you can't get up or down on your own.

"So how much damage did the fire do?" Cora Lee spoke up. We all were very curious to know.

"I'm sorry to say the kitchen was heavily damaged," Frank reported. "It was contained there, but there is smoke and water damage to the dining room. we hope to have something in place in the next day or two to feed you. We're just not sure how we're going to handle it yet. But you can be certain that your meal service will continue in some form until the kitchen can be rebuilt."

"So how did the fire start?" Cora Lee demanded.

"We don't have information on that until the fire marshal is able to get in there to investigate and make his report. Unfortunately, one of our residents was injured and has been taken to the hospital."

"Who?" I asked.

"Arthur Tisdale."

Cora Lee was standing beside me. "See?" she hissed in my ear. "I knew he was going to have something to do with this. Mark my words, he probably set it."

I tried to ignore her. She was great at jumping to conclusions before she knew the facts. "How badly was he hurt?" I asked Frank.

"We don't know at this point. And as you know we can't comment on the condition of a resident because of HIPAA standards anyway."

The rules of privacy had their point, but it was always frustrating when we wanted to know about the condition of a fellow resident.

As soon as I got back to my apartment I called Ty.

"Well, that was an adventure," I said when he answered.

"I can do without that kind of adventure, thank you. How did you fare on your side?"

"The wine was flowing, and there was a party atmosphere until it dragged on and on. Then we all ran out of steam and just wanted to get home to our beds."

"Pretty much the same here. A couple of people brought out some hard liquor and a couple of people got a little rowdy. But we, too, were ready for it to end."

"Did you hear the kitchen was destroyed?"

"Yeah, I did. And did you hear that Arthur Tisdale was hurt?"

"Yes, they told us. But nothing about his condition. I don't think I know him," I said.

"He's from my wing. I know him slightly. Strange dude."

"Cora Lee says he's had a vendetta against the kitchen staff. Complains all the time about the food. She's sure he set the fire."

"I wouldn't believe anything Cora Lee says."

"I'll never take her word, but on the other hand there might be some truth in it."

"I'm so tired right now I don't care. We can discuss it tomorrow."

"Okay, Ty. See you in exercise class."

FOURTEEN

A SHORT ARTICLE on the fire was in the morning paper on a back page but it gave little detail other than the authorities were trying to determine how it started. It did state that one resident had been injured but not the extent of his injuries.

The TV news had little more information than that. It did mention Arthur's name but only that he was being treated in a local hospital.

When I came downstairs for exercise class in the morning the acrid stench from the fire was almost overpowering. As I passed by the glass-paned doors to the dining room I could hear the roar of the fans set up around the perimeter to dry out the carpet. The tables and chairs had been removed, and I could see black streaks on the smoke-stained walls. It was heartbreaking though I realized it could have been so much worse.

When I got to the community room where the exercise classes are held Spunky was at the door to explain that classes had been canceled.

"They're going to set up this room for dining while the other one is being repaired," she said.

"But how are they going to prepare food?" I asked.

"They've made arrangements with a catering company."

Ty showed up and she repeated the news to him.

"Oh, boy," he said, "I guess we'll have to work out on the exercise equipment if we want to maintain our model-like physiques." He held up his arm and ostentatiously squeezed his invisible bicep. "Well, it was there yesterday. Where did it go?"

Joining in the fun I added, "Yes, if I want to continue to wear my bikini I guess I'll have to do that too."

"I challenge you to a race on the treadmills," he said.

"You're on."

Our exercise room has two side-by-side treadmills with a number of other machines suitable for seniors. They are often in use, but this day no one else was in the room. They were probably recovering from the shock of last night's fire.

We mounted our respective treadmills and set the speed to a quick but not exhausting pace. Since we were alone we could talk without worrying about being overheard.

"So tell me what you know about Arthur Tisdale," I said.

"You've seen the TV chef Gordon Ramsay who screams at the poor contestants?"

"Yeah, I think so. At least I've seen previews of the show. I don't watch those programs because I don't like to cook as you well know."

"Well, Arthur sort of reminds me of him. I'm surprised you haven't noticed him in the dining room giving the servers a fit over the food."

"Well, there are always the complainers so I guess he didn't stand out."

"We haven't been in the dining room when he's been on one of his worst rampages. But I've heard about them."

"So why didn't he take his complaints to the Dining Committee?"

"Apparently he has. But he didn't think it made enough difference."

"So do you think it's possible he set the fire?"

"Anything's possible. But I can't imagine anyone over-reacting to that degree."

"You know what? I'm not as charitable as you. I'm willing to believe anything if someone can prove it."

"What? Are you thinking of investigating this now?" Ty turned to look at me and almost lost his footing on the moving belt.

"Watch out there, Buddy, before you fall off," I cautioned.

He stared straight ahead at the wall. "I'm just wondering if you're getting addicted to this sleuthing business. We haven't made any progress with Lawrence and Deborah's case. Why are you so intrigued with this?"

I shrugged. "I'm just ruminating, Ty. You know, like a cow I'm chewing my cud and thinking aloud. It's just that I live here and this has affected me personally."

"Well, whatever. I think our first case should be our priority. So, what are we going to do about that?"

"I don't know," I had to admit.

After our stint on the treadmills we went around the room and tried out some of the other machines designed to strengthen various muscles. Spunky had worked with each resident when we first moved in to demonstrate how they worked and to set up a safe but gradually more difficult schedule for us to pursue. Unfortunately neither of us had done this. So we were still at the basic level.

"Now that we can't have exercise class I think we should make it a habit to come here every morning and work out," Ty said. "See if we can make some progress on these machines."

"Not nearly as much fun as working out with Spunky, but I guess we have to do what we have to do. I may do laps afterward as well. Got to keep in shape for the Masters."

"I'm no swimmer but maybe I'll splash around a little if you promise not to make fun of me."

"Who? *Me?* I wouldn't do a thing like that."

"Of course not. What was I thinking?"

It was time for lunch so we decided to go back to the Community Room and see how the meal service was going to work out.

They had set up folding tables and chairs throughout the room with a buffet lunch set out on the far right side. I assumed that our nice dining room furniture had been damaged and needed to be restored. Already a long line had formed at the buffet table. We had become spoiled with sit-down service. I knew we weren't going to like this very much. Well, at least I wouldn't. Ty is more laid-back than I am.

The line wound its way slowly around the perimeter of the room and we finally got to the food. It was a selection of three kinds of sandwiches, a large bowl of mixed greens salad with two bowls of dressing to choose from and some brownies for dessert. It was obvious we weren't going to go hungry, but it was certainly uninspired.

Ty and I hunted around for two seats at the same table. We were accustomed to sitting at a "two-top" in the dining room where we could be alone to discuss our latest investigation. There was nothing here but tables shoved together to seat eight or twelve.

We finally found two seats at a table populated mostly with residents from the East Wing where Ty lives. I found myself next to Ginger Willard, the resident with the foul-mouthed parrot. Actually, this was her second one. Her first one had died quite suddenly in the spring, and when Ty and I were on our way to comfort her we ran into Phyllis Duncan standing in the middle of the hall holding a bloody knife. We later learned her husband was dead on their living room floor. This event launched our first investigation which eventually exonerated Phyllis.

But, back to Ginger. Her parrot Lester spewed profanity it had learned from her late husband. She tolerated it, even welcomed it because it reminded her of her dearly departed mate. Eventually she got a replacement she called Jester, and I had hoped she'd instruct it to sing or recite poetry or mimic something innocuous. But no, she taught it all the naughty words the first parrot had spouted just so it would bring back memories of her husband. This whole incident taught me not to underestimate the amount of weirdness that can go on in a retirement home. Whether brought on by incipient dementia, or just the slow accretion of peculiar habits and personality tics over the years I'm not sure. But it's never boring.

"So how are you, Ginger?" I asked.

"I'm good, Vi. Did I tell you that I purchased a memorial bench in memory of my dear Lester?" Memorial benches paid for by the spouses of newly departed residents are placed around our campus, a nice spot to sit and contemplate nature. This was the first one dedicated to a bird.

"Oh," I said startled and trying not to laugh. "That's nice." I couldn't think of another thing to say.

"Yes, it's directly opposite where I buried Lester over in the woods. So I can sit there and conjure up my happy memories of him."

I wondered if she gave half as much thought to her departed husband whose memory the parrot was supposed to invoke.

I wanted to change the subject before I said something I'd regret so I asked her how she made out during the fire the night before.

"I was so worried about Jester that I couldn't wait to get

back to my apartment. I'd have just died if anything had happened to him so soon after Lester's demise."

"He was okay wasn't he?"

"Sort of. He does get nervous if I'm gone for any length of time. It takes him some time to calm down when I come back. He didn't settle down for at least a couple of hours. Damn Arthur Tisdale's soul."

I looked at her in shock. Even though her parrots used foul language that was the first time I'd heard as much as a "damn" from Ginger. "Why do you say that?"

"Everybody knows Arthur set that fire." She gave me a rather imperious look as though to ask why was I so out of the loop?

"And what do you base this on?" I stared back steadily to see if she would back pedal on her statement.

She suddenly took great interest in her meal and began to eat some salad. After a couple of minutes, apparently unable to come up with a good answer, she shrugged and said, "Because he said he'd just as soon burn down the place the food was so lousy."

"Just because he *said* it doesn't mean he *did* it," I argued. "That would never fly in court."

She laid her fork down and turned to me. "You know he got burned, Don't you? So he must have been there. What would he be doing in the kitchen after the dinner hour unless he was up to no good?"

She had me there.

FIFTEEN

Ty AND I decided to visit Cliff after lunch. We hoped he'd be out of intensive care and in a regular room by now. When we inquired about him at the front desk we learned he'd been moved to a private room. Following the receptionist's directions we finally found our way there. Greta was sitting beside him, of course, but she looked a little more rested than she had before.

"You're looking good," I said to Cliff though he still looked pale and drawn but definitely better than he had the last time we saw him.

"Not quite ready to kick butt yet, but making progress." He grinned. "At least I have a few less tubes and monitors."

"He's getting pretty antsy," Greta said. "Wants me to bring him his briefcase so he can do some work."

"For Pete's sake," Ty said. "Take advantage of this opportunity to slack off. You might not get another chance in quite a while."

"That's the problem," Greta said. "Cliff doesn't know how to slow down. I'm sure he has adult ADHD, wants to be doing something every minute. He worries about his clients."

Ty shook his head. "I'm sure they're in good hands until you can get back in the saddle." He was standing by the bed and he patted Cliff's hand. I thought it seemed a bit patronizing, but I wasn't going to say so. Ty's heart was in the right place.

"He thinks no one can do as well for them as he can," Greta said.

Ty immediately launched into the story of last night's fire. Evidently he was afraid I would accidently say something I'd regret about trying to help one of his clients.

"Good lord!" Greta exclaimed. "Do you know how it started?"

"There's not been any official word. But the residents seem to think one of the guys there did it," I said.

"Why would they think that?" Cliff asked.

"He's a former chef and apparently he complained all the time about the food. Someone actually heard him say he might as well burn down the kitchen."

Lawyer through and through, Cliff perked up. "Well, that's not enough to charge him. But it sounds like it's worth looking into."

"I suppose so," Ty answered.

"Sounds like it's right up your alley," Cliff continued. "You guys certainly outfoxed me last spring. Why don't you bring your talents to solve this?"

I wondered if this was a ploy to make sure we didn't get involved in the death of Jeremy Scofield. At least it was verification he didn't know we already were.

"I'm sure the fire marshal is on the case," I said.

We chatted for a little while longer but I was worried about overtiring him so I finally said, "Hey, Ty, don't you have some errands to run?"

He looked at me blankly and finally seemed to catch on. "Oh, yes, the drugstore and the post office. Always something."

I put my arm through his and led him out the door after we said our goodbyes. "We don't need to wear him out," I cautioned in a low voice. "Even though he seems eager to talk, I think we need to keep our visits short and sweet."

"You're right. Nudge me with your elbow next time."

We'd gotten to the lobby when an idea occurred to me.

"Wait a sec," I said to Ty. "I want to ask the lady at the desk a question."

Leaving him in the middle of the room I walked over to the receptionist. "I'm looking for Arthur Tisdale. Can you tell me his room number?" I had no idea if he was in this hospital or not, but this seemed like a good way to find out.

She consulted her computer. "He's in the burn unit," she said.

"Can he have visitors?"

"Not at this time," she said.

Was he in such bad shape he couldn't have visitors, or under guard because he was suspected of setting the fire?

I relayed this information to Ty. "What do you think?" I asked.

"I think we have enough on our hands trying to help Lawrence and Deborah. Besides, if Arthur is incommunicado there isn't much we could find out anyway."

"I guess you're right. So what do we do next?"

"Before all hell broke loose at GH we discussed talking to some of the people at the TV station where Jeremy worked. Why don't we do that?"

"Oh, yeah. I'd forgotten about that. Do we just walk in and collar people?" I asked.

"I'm not sure that would produce results. We need some kind of cover story like you used with Suzi Wallace."

"Being in the news business, they probably know everyone at the *Guilford Gossip*. I doubt I could get away with that."

"How about saying you're writing a book about the murder, planning to follow it through the trial and all."

I thought about that for a few minutes. "Do you think that would fly?"

"I don't know why not. It seems every other person is writing a book these days. If they ask who your publisher is, say you're writing it on spec and if no publisher wants it you can always publish it yourself."

"Hey, that's a thought."

"Okay, Vi, don't get carried away. This is just your cover."

"Spoilsport."

We decided it was too late to try to start anything today so instead we opted to drive west to a barbeque chicken place we'd been to once before. It was at least an hour's drive but well worth it. Ostensibly in Cleveland, NC but actually on a back winding road in the middle of nowhere, it's a nondescript cinder block building next to a gravel parking lot with a hand painted sign that says "No Log Trucks." Keaton's has been serving loyal customers for half a century with chicken that is deep fried then immersed in a cauldron of hot barbeque sauce.

We ordered at the small counter before sitting in one of the booths. Talk about no frills. The interior was wood-paneled with several horizontal mirrors emulating a window in the windowless restaurant. The meals soon arrived on paper plates covered with a sheet of wax paper. Since I can't tolerate very hot food I had a "mild upper" (meaning breast and wings) while Ty had a "hot lower," legs and thighs. We had sides of soul food, mac and cheese, baked beans and slaw (hot sauce or mayo) and of course sweet tea.

"Oh my god," Ty swooned after a bite of chicken, "If only we could get them to come and cook our meals at GH."

I was feeling like I'd died and gone to heaven. "Man, wouldn't that be great?" Even Ty succumbed and ordered dessert, sweet potato pie, while I had the red velvet cake.

We were feeling mellow on the ride home, glad we didn't have to stand in line to get our dinner and full of one of the best meals we'd ever had.

"If that place was only closer, I'd come here every day," I said. "At least until the kitchen is rebuilt."

Ty took his eyes off the road for a minute to look me up and down. "I think you're a very nice size now, Vi. But I wouldn't recommend that. Can you imagine the calories we consumed?"

"Some days I wish I'd never heard of the word calorie. It sure takes the fun out of life."

"You're right. My bad."

Since the next day was Saturday we decided to postpone going to the TV station until the first of the week.

We got home too late to hear the six o'clock news so I watched it at ten o'clock. They reported the fire inspector had confirmed that the kitchen fire at GH had been set but currently there was no person of interest.

How strange is that? I wondered. Since Arthur Tisdale was burned in the fire it seemed logical he would be connected to it. But apparently they didn't yet have enough evidence to tie him to it. And somehow I couldn't believe anyone living here could even think of endangering the lives of the other residents.

SIXTEEN

TY PLAYED MARATHON bridge most of the day on Saturday. I spent the time cleaning out drawers and cupboards in my kitchen. Considering the fact I do so little cooking, it's amazing just how jumbled and messy they can get. I have a habit of throwing pans into the lower cabinets because they aren't that easy for me to reach any more, and suddenly I realized everything in there was liable to come toppling onto the floor the next time I opened a door. I decided to stack my pans in my oven where I'd have easier access. Why not? After all, I don't bake anymore. The microwave is my cooking tool of choice the few times I cook at all. I'm not sure why I even hang onto my pans except for the once-in-a-blue-moon occasion.

Once that was accomplished I moved on to the bedroom. My walk-in closet (my favorite thing about this whole apartment) has become my go-to place for storage until it is now "barely-step-in" instead of "walk-in." Even though I brought little with me when I moved from Maine, my belongings must be fertile and are multiplying at an alarming rate. Where does all this stuff come from? I managed to fill two large trash bags with stuff to go to Goodwill.

When I finally had all the domesticity I could stomach I headed for the pool to do laps. Forty-five minutes in the pool and ten in the spa and I was a new woman, relatively speaking.

Rather than spend time waiting in line for our supper

Ty and I decided to go to Panera's. We knew it would be too expensive to continue to eat our meals out, but we were hoping they'd work the kinks out of the temporary setup in the next day or so.

"So are you ready to go to the TV station Monday morning?" Ty asked after we got to a table.

"I've been too busy to give it much thought yet."

"Busy? What do you have to be busy about?"

I sat silently for a couple of minutes trying to temper my reply. "Just because they feed us and dust and sweep once a week doesn't mean there's nothing to do around my apartment. I did some cleaning in my kitchen and my bedroom."

I could tell by the look on his face he realized how he sounded. Though he doesn't actually blush, his ears turn red when he feels embarrassed. "Um, sorry," he said. "That didn't come out quite right."

"No, it didn't."

"I meant to ask were you busy doing something fun?"

I laughed. "I should make you squirm some more, Ty. But you're so transparent I don't have the heart."

He grinned sheepishly. "Sometimes my tongue gets the better of me. Truce?"

"Truce."

We decided to get together Sunday after brunch and plan more about our approach to the TV station.

THINGS SEEMED SLIGHTLY better organized by Sunday brunch. The staff had made robo calls to all residents setting a time period for us to go to the Community Room to eat. They explained it was the only way to ensure it wouldn't be overcrowded. Ty and I found out we were scheduled for slots a half an hour apart: he was scheduled for 12:15 and I was scheduled for 12:45, but he found someone on his floor who was glad to exchange places with him in order to eat earlier.

The line was much shorter as a result and we were actually able to find a spot for two in a far corner.

The menu consisted of fried chicken, mashed potatoes and green beans with cookies for dessert. Not really a brunch as we usually had breakfast items to choose from as well as entrees and vegetables. But I guess that was more than the caterer could do.

"Do you think Kentucky Fried Chicken catered the meal today?" I asked.

"Probably not. After going to Keaton's this chicken tastes like old cardboard."

I sighed. "Well, we're not going to starve. But I hope it doesn't take too long to get our kitchen repaired."

"I'm not optimistic about that."

"Let's change the subject. It's too depressing."

"Okay. What's our plan for tomorrow?"

"I think we need to call first and find out what's the best time to talk to some of the news staff." I wiped my greasy hands on a paper napkin. I couldn't tackle the chicken breast with knife and fork so I gave up and ate it with my fingers.

"Do you think they'd refuse to meet with us?"

"I don't think so. Most people are flattered when they're told they're being interviewed for a book."

"How do you know that?"

"I had a friend in Maine who was a writer. She said no one ever turned her down when she told them she needed their expertise. Especially if you say you'll give them an acknowledgement."

"'Knavery and flattery are blood relations.'"

"What? Surely you didn't make that up," I said.

"No. Abe Lincoln did. It fits doesn't it?" I forgot that

Ty is a voracious reader of history. He also has a remarkable memory.

"Well, my intentions are on the side of the angels...I hope," I added.

"I guess we won't know till it's all over."

"And even then the outcome might not be the right one unfortunately."

We discussed whether or not Ty should go with me.

"Don't you think that would be a little awkward?" he said. "How would you explain me?"

"Why couldn't we be writing this 'book' as a team? It's not all that unusual. I'd really feel more comfortable if you were there. You'd think of questions that I missed and vice versa."

Ty dunked his partially dried-out cookie in his coffee leaving crumbs floating unappetizingly on the surface, I don't usually forego dessert, but I pushed aside my cookie when I saw that. Cardboard chicken was bad enough. I didn't need cardboard cookies too. "If you think that would work it's okay with me. But you take the lead. If you had a writer friend you might be better faking it than I would."

That was a cop-out but I wasn't going to complain as long as he'd come with me. I told him I'd call the station in the morning and set up a time and let him know.

THE CHANNEL 6 receptionist told me that the best time to come would be around one or one-thirty.

"They'll be back from lunch then and won't have to be on camera till the five o'clock news."

"So do we just show up?"

"Sure. When you get here, I'll check and see who's free to talk to you."

Ty and I decided to eat lunch at a McDonald's close to the station to make sure we could get there on time. Eating at GH was a crap shoot now as to when you might get through the line.

I opted for Micky D's new chocolate chip frappe and assuaged my conscience by getting a junior cheeseburger and a fruit and walnut salad. Ty, claiming he wasn't very hungry, had a small bowl of chili and a regular coffee.

"Have you thought of what you're going to ask?" Ty asked. I think he was nervous about these interviews which was strange because he'd never been like that before.

"Not really. I like to wing it."

"Well I hope I can wing it with you. These people are not like most we've interviewed in the past. They do it for a living. They will probably be a lot more wary and far less naïve. I'm sure they have good bullshit detectors."

I frowned. "I just want to get some answers to Jeremy's murder."

"But you're telling them you're a writer. That's not exactly a fact."

"If I told them I was a cop or an investigator I think I'd be out of bounds. But this is a small fib for the greater good. I guess I *could* try to write a book if I wanted to."

He settled back in his seat and gave me a small smile. "Well, if you can rationalize it, I guess I can too."

Since we're both a bit neurotic when it comes to being places on time we were at the station at 12:59. I introduced us to the receptionist and reminded her of my call.

"Oh, yes," she said. "If you'll just take a seat over there I'll see who's free to talk to you."

We waited about fifteen minutes before a stylish-looking woman came out of the offices and walked toward us. I'd guess she was in her early forties, her black hair cut in a short bob and wearing sensible though good-looking pumps. Several strands of necklaces made of colored glass beads made her long-sleeved white silk shirt and black flared skirt just dressy enough. Her demeanor was all business. She put out her hand as she greeted me. "I'm Vanessa Anderson. I produce the six o'clock news."

Ty and I scrambled to our feet to shake her hand. I introduced us both. "We're working on a book about Jeremy Scofield's murder and would appreciate it if we could ask you a few questions."

I hadn't been nervous beforehand but now my knees were quaking. Could we really pull this off?

She asked us to follow her to her office which was down a side hall. It wasn't large, but it was impressive in its own way. A wall of photographs of station personnel posed with celebrities overlooked piles of books and papers scattered everywhere. On the other wall was a shelf holding local and regional Emmys and other awards.

Vanessa had to pull in an extra guest chair from an adjoining office to accommodate us both. Once we were seated she said, "Isn't it a little odd to be writing about a murder that is still under investigation? Don't writers normally wait until someone is convicted and sentenced before they do their research?"

That came out of left field. I gripped the arms of the chair hard as I tried to form an answer that sounded plausible. "I thought we could get a head start by getting background information on Scofield for one thing. Since the victim was a well-known figure and a couple in high standing in the community has been charged, it seems the story will be very compelling no matter the outcome."

"Yes," Ty chimed in, "we feel there's so much drama involved it makes a great tale already."

Vanessa was now staring at me, and I was becoming increasingly uncomfortable.

"Aren't you one of the women who discovered Jeremy's body?"

It had been more than two weeks and I didn't think anyone would remember me from that brief mention on TV at the time of the murder. I should have realized that this woman was steeped in the news and probably had a memory like an elephant. I felt like she'd caught me with my hand in the cookie jar. My thoughts were racing a mile a minute trying to think how to answer her.

I sat up straighter. "I am," I said. "I was so traumatized by that experience I've tended to dwell on it, and I've had trouble sleeping. I realized that writing about it might help drive out the demons. I think it will be therapeutic."

She nodded. "Have you lined up a publisher?"

"No, it's too early to do that. The case has to proceed further, I believe, before I can get a publisher interested."

"Okay." She leaned back in her chair and took a sip out of a cup that sat on her desk. "Oh, sorry," she said, "can I get you two some coffee?"

"I'm fine," I said.

"Me too," Ty added.

"So what exactly do you want to know?"

SEVENTEEN

I FELT AS though I'd been perched precariously at the edge of a cliff and someone grabbed my coattails and pulled me back to safety. I reached into my large pocketbook on the floor beside me and pulled out a notebook and pen. I didn't want to get caught without one like I did interviewing Suzi Wallace. This woman would know I was a fake in a minute.

I relaxed back into my chair. "Can you tell me how Jeremy was viewed here at the station? You were here when he worked at Channel 6, weren't you?"

Vanessa picked up a pen and tapped it thoughtfully against her lips. "Are you going to quote me on this or will it be an anonymous statement?"

It was beginning to seem that no one was willing to discuss Jeremy Scofield publicly. "Which would you prefer?"

"If you want me to be perfectly honest I don't want my name used. Now that the poor man is dead it might be regarded as unseemly to say negative things. However, there's not a whole lot positive that I can say."

This was better than I expected. I thought the staff here might close ranks to protect their own. As with Suzi Wallace, it didn't matter to me if she wanted to claim it came from an anonymous source. I made a point to write everything she said in my notebook the way a real author would. I wondered if I should have brought something to record her, but it was too late for that.

"Public figures are open to scrutiny as far as I'm concerned," Ty said. "If they don't like people looking into their personal lives they shouldn't take on that kind of a job."

"I'm not sure I agree with you one hundred percent," Vanessa said. "Politicians yes. They work for all of us and we want to know everything about them in order to make intelligent decisions when we vote. Other people, like movie stars for instance, don't owe the public anything. Their private lives should be private."

"I agree," I said. "I don't know where TV anchors are on that spectrum. I don't think their private lives should be scrutinized if they're just doing their job. But Jeremy is dead under very mysterious circumstances, and in order for my readers to understand what led to this terrible end, I think they have to know the man."

"Nicely put," Vanessa said smiling at me. Again I felt I'd been put to the test, and while I was afraid for a minute Ty had opened up a can of worms, it turned out positive. She took another sip of her coffee and then picked up the pen again and tapped it on her desk. I figured the pen must serve as a touchstone for her.

"Jeremy was not a nice guy. He was a skirt chaser even though he was married. But that wasn't the worst thing he ever did."

"So the worst thing was…?" Ty asked.

"Well, of course hitting that woman while he was drunk. But what the public doesn't know is he started a non-profit organization to raise money for histiocytosis X."

"Histio what?" I asked.

"It's some kind of autoimmune disease that often strikes children. It's a terrible thing. Children often die very young. Since most people have never heard of it, it's a worthy cause…if it's for real."

"What do you mean?" I asked.

"Jeremy claimed he had a young niece with the disease and that's why he started this foundation. But I got suspicious about it and started to do a little checking. I could never find he had a niece, let alone a sick one, and I felt sure that most of the money went into his own pocket. In fact I had even contacted the state attorney general about it just before Jeremy hit that woman and ended up in jail. I guess the investigation was dropped at that point. At least I never heard any more about it."

"Wow," I said. "What was he thinking? I mean didn't he make pretty good money as an anchor?"

"In our smaller market he did okay. Nothing like the network anchors of course. But Amy loved to spend it faster than he could make it. I guess he thought he had to keep her happy by giving her all the money she wanted so she'd overlook his philandering."

"I wonder how she made out while he was in prison?" Ty asked.

"Probably lived off what he had made through the charity."

"So what was the name of this so-called charity?" I asked thinking that might give us some leads if we could find anyone else associated with it.

"Would you believe 'The X Factor'? The TV program was popular in England at that time but hadn't yet begun in the US. I guess he thought it was a catchy name."

"How do you get away with something like that…I mean soliciting money for a good cause but pocketing it instead?" I asked.

"It's not too difficult especially if you solicit online. There's no absolute overseer of charitable organizations. And if you claim to make less than $25,000 a year you don't even have to report to the IRS."

"Do you think he took in less than that?" Ty asked.

Vanessa rolled her eyes. "Do I look that naïve?"

"So the bottom line here is you really have to check out organizations you donate to," I said. "Looks like I'll have to do some research on that end. I'll need to prove he was skimming or I guess Amy could sue me if I put it in print." I was trying to sound like an authentic author. In reality she'd given me enough to start checking it out.

"You could probably say there were rumors to that effect without getting into trouble," Vanessa said. "But maybe you should get some legal advice if you do get published."

"We'll definitely check into that," Ty said.

"Is there anything else you can tell us?" I asked. "I don't want to impose on your time. You're very generous to meet with us this way."

"Can't think of anything in particular. Jeremy made plenty of enemies, so although they've arrested the Rineharts, it could easily have been someone else as far as motive is concerned. Of course the evidence is pretty damning I'll have to admit."

Ty stood up so I followed his lead. He reached out to shake Vanessa's hand. "You've been quite a help. We appreciate that you've taken the time to meet with us."

"Yes," I added. "And we'll certainly give you credit if it gets into publication."

"Please don't," she said. "I don't want my name anywhere near this book."

Well, so much for the great incentive. But she was glad to talk to us anyway which was all that counted.

On our way back to GH we discussed everything we'd learned.

"Do you imagine someone who gave to his fund-raiser could have killed him?" Ty asked.

"You mean when they found out the money didn't go where it was supposed to?"

"Yeah."

"I think you'd have to lose a pot full of money before you'd be mad enough to do something like that."

"Who knows what can set some people off?"

EIGHTEEN

WHEN WE GOT back to GH Ty said he wanted to check out some things on his computer. "I'd like to see if the website is still up for Jeremy's fund-raiser. See if it lists any other names connected with it."

I elected to swim laps in the pool and do some reading before we met for dinner.

Not surprisingly we'd been assigned different times for the evening meal. I was scheduled for 5:30 while Ty's time was 6:15. He found another resident who was supposed to eat at the earlier time and was delighted to permanently exchange places with him claiming she was used to eating late.

The buffet service went a little smoother, but the food was still uninspired and made me appreciate even more the meals we had before the fire destroyed the kitchen. I wondered how the work was progressing on rebuilding it, but we couldn't get near it to find out. We could only hear the muffled sound of pounding and sawing when we came down the hallway beside the dining room. On the other hand, the walls in the dining room had been freshly painted and the carpet cleaned, waiting for the furniture to return.

Once we were seated I asked Ty if he had learned anything about The X Factor.

"Well, of course now with the popular TV show, the first umpteen Google hits referred to it. I finally found something way down the list that mentioned a charity. But when I pulled it up, it said the website was 'under construction.' Not quite sure what that means. It could have been a way to close it down when he went to jail or it might mean he was trying to resurrect it."

"Hmm. That's interesting."

"Sure wish we could talk to Amy," Ty said. He seemed to have trouble accepting that she was off limits.

"Not only have the cops probably told her not to talk to anyone as I said before, it would get back to Cliff for sure if we tried to meet with her. Anyway, if she was living high off the contributions, do you think she'd ever admit it? She'd claim she knew nothing about it."

"Say, speaking of Cliff, maybe we ought to go see him this evening. It's been several days and I figure he'll go home tomorrow or the day after."

"You're right," I said. "I've been distracted. We haven't seen him since Friday and he'll wonder where we've been."

We left as soon as we'd finished eating. Though it had been a very hot day, a cool breeze made the ride in Ty's car more pleasurable than it had been in some weeks.

"Everything is beginning to look pretty brown," I said as we passed lawns suffering from lack of rain. "I noticed we're about five inches below normal rainfall for the year."

"Yeah, what we need is a hurricane."

"Ty!" I cried. "What about the poor people on the coast?" Hurricanes can drop much needed rain as far inland as the foothills but they can devastate the eastern portion of the state first. One or two have even meandered up through the mountains before they fizzled out.

"Well, I would hope it would pass through an uninhabited area and not do too much damage while it brings us the rain we need."

Ty had not lived in North Carolina when some of the worst hurricanes have come through and obviously wasn't aware of their capacity to wreak havoc. I'd heard tales from Greta and Cliff about the destruction the winds bring and the severe flooding that comes from the lingering rain. Many people don't realize flooding can cause more deaths and damage than the wind itself.

"That's not likely to happen," I said. "If it comes this far inland, you know the coast is going to suffer big time. Don't ever wish for one of those. But a good soaking rain would be nice."

"Mea culpa. I guess I spoke before I thought."

I wanted to say *a habit of yours* but I didn't.

When we got to his room we found Cliff looking quite chipper. I was surprised at how fast he had bounced back from surgery.

"I get to go home tomorrow," he said beaming.

"Fantastic," I said.

"The problem will be holding him down," Greta complained. "I know he's itching to get back to work though the doc says he can't go to the office for another six weeks. And he'll have to come back to the hospital for some therapy as well. I hope that will keep him out of trouble."

"I promise to behave." Cliff had a twinkle in his eye which made me doubt the truth of that.

"I'm sure the office can get along all right without you," I said.

Cliff scowled. "Well, thanks a lot."

And I fussed at Ty for speaking before he thought. "Oh, Cliff, you know I didn't mean it that way. I know they miss you a lot. But your health is the most important consideration." I turned into a chatterbox trying to undo my faux pas.

"Amen, Vi," Greta added. "The office is much better off without you for a short period while you recover,

Cliff. Think what kind of shape it would be in permanently because you worked yourself to death."

"Okay, okay," Cliff raised his hands in surrender. "I'll be good." He sounded like he meant it.

We chatted for a while about the state of the GH kitchen and the weather before we said our goodbyes.

I stopped at the receptionist's desk on the way out of the hospital to ask again about Arthur Tisdale.

"Sorry. No visitors are allowed," she said.

I realized we hadn't heard a thing yet about the fire. How had they managed to keep it so quiet? While they'd announced it had been set almost immediately afterward, they'd never identified a person of interest. I wondered why.

The next morning Ty and I had coffee before we went to the exercise room to work out on the treadmills and other equipment. It gave us a chance to review what we might do during the day to further our investigation.

I said, "You know, Leah Rinehart started us down this path and we haven't talked to her in quite a while. How about meeting with her so we can tell her what all we've learned so far and see if any of it triggers any ideas or reminds her of something we don't know."

"Sure. Why don't you find out if we can see her this afternoon?"

I phoned her as soon as I got back to my apartment.

"I'm so glad you called, Vi. I kept hoping I'd hear what you've learned about Jeremy's death. But I didn't want to bug you."

The underlying tone was slightly petulant. She wanted me to know I'd hurt her feelings. Well, it couldn't be helped.

"I'm sorry, Leah. All kinds of hell have broken loose

this past week. Did you know Cliff Holcomb had a heart attack?"

"Oh my god no. That doesn't bode well for Lawrence and Deborah."

"He had surgery last week. He's doing well and is going home today."

"Why didn't you call and tell me?" she asked sounding even more upset.

That got my back up. "Because I've been so busy looking into Jeremy's death, Leah. I've been running around interviewing people, and on top of that there was a fire here at GH."

"I'm sorry," she said in a contrite voice. "It's just that I'm on such pins and needles. I remember now reading about the fire. How bad was it?"

"Let's wait till we can come over and see you. We'll fill you in on everything then."

"I'll be home all day. Why don't you come after lunch?"

"Sounds good. How about two?"

"Great. See you then."

Ty and I met for lunch at our customary time but the line was much longer than normal. The caterer had been late setting up, and we stood in line an extra twenty minutes. I figured this would be the norm until the kitchen was finished, and we might as well get used to it. But that didn't stop us from getting fidgety as we inched along. I realized how much I appreciated the fact that our meals were served to us when we ate in the dining room. I'm not a patient person and I hate waiting in lines. Ty isn't much better and I heard him mumble, "When the heck are they going to get that kitchen done?"

I chose to ignore him because no one had the answer to that.

We finally got through the line and sat down to eat our

barbeque sandwiches and potato chips and butterscotch pudding. Not even a salad.

"Good gosh, Ty. How can I ever keep my 'trim' figure when we have to eat all these calories?" I asked him tongue-in-cheek.

He looked at me askance. "You're kidding I hope."

"Well, I was giving some thought to going on a diet."

"Your nose is growing, Vi."

"Spoilsport."

We finally got around to talking about our visit to Leah.

"Are we going to tell her everything we've learned?" Ty asked.

"I don't see any reason not to. She might be able to add something. I'm especially anxious to find out if she knows anything about Jeremy's fund-raiser."

"Oh, right."

With our delayed lunch we had no time to spare to get to Leah's house. She greeted us with such enthusiasm I figured she was making up for her sulkiness over the phone.

"Come in, come in," she cooed hugging each of us as if we were long lost buddies. I guessed that since we'd talked to her she realized that we were the only ones who could fill her in on what was happening. There had been no news about the investigation in the newspaper because essentially nothing was happening on the case as far as the public could know. With Cliff laid up I doubted much was going on with the defense either.

"I've got some green iced tea," she said when we sat down. "Can I get you some?"

I could detect a flicker of a grimace on Ty's face. I knew he hated green tea, thought it tasted like "something you'd use to clean the kitchen floor with." But he quickly smiled. "None for me. Just came from lunch."

"I'll have some, thanks." Though I don't generally lean

toward the more healthy foods, I've taken a liking to it. And it was so blessed hot out I craved liquid all the time.

She went into the kitchen and came back with two glasses and handed one to me. She settled into a chair opposite us, took a sip from her glass, and said, "Now bring me up to date, please," emphasizing the please. Obviously she was going to make nice.

So I began by telling her I'd met with Suzi Wallace, Amy Scofield's sister, Missy Fenstermacher and Candice Knowlton.

"Suzi Wallace? Some years ago, before we divorced, we got together with Jeremy and his wife and Suzi and her husband. Then it was like she and her husband fell off the face of the earth. I never knew what happened to them. Jeremy was always vague when I'd ask about them and say that they'd had a little falling-out or something."

"It was way more than that," I said. "Since she was open about it to me I guess I can share it with you. The two couples went to a Christmas party at the station together. Everyone was totally wasted and Jeremy managed to get Suzi off in a small room where they had sex. She felt he took advantage of her inebriated condition, that she was too far gone to resist. Anyway, her husband found out and divorced her."

Leah shook her head. "I should have known. Once a scumbag always a scumbag."

"She says her sister never found out about it, but she was aware of his other affairs. She always blames it on the women."

"I don't get women like that. How can anyone be so blind?"

Ty had been silent all this time. "That's known as desperation. You're so afraid of being alone you'll do anything to hang onto the wretch no matter what."

"Like being alone is so bad," I said. "It definitely has its compensations."

"Here, here," said Ty.

NINETEEN

"SO YOU SAID you talked to Missy Fenstermacher," Leah said.

"Yes, I interviewed her because we were trying to find Rosalind Voncannon and Deborah said she was the one who knew her best."

"You couldn't find Rosalind?"

"Lawrence fired her. Didn't you know?"

"No! Well, it was about time. I thought she should have been fired long ago. But he's too softhearted."

"Apparently she made quite a scene when she left. And some people wondered if she and Jeremy were having an affair. No one seems to know."

"I've tried everything I know to run her down," Ty said. "The computer can be a useful tool for that but I came up zilch. Her phone service has been discontinued, her place is for rent. She told people she might go out west but nobody knows where."

"That sounds suspicious, doesn't it?" asked Leah.

"Maybe," said Ty. "But what would killing Jeremy have to do with being fired? Perhaps she did have an affair with Jeremy that went bad so she killed him and then planted the evidence which would land Lawrence in jail for a long time. Killing two birds with one stone so to speak. But that's a lot of 'ifs.'"

Leah looked thoughtful. "You've definitely made some inroads, don't you think?."

"It's all hypothesis. We don't have any concrete evidence," Ty said.

"So did Missy tell you anything helpful?"

"Not really," I said.

"What about Candy?"

"I talked to her on the phone. It sounded like she had a house full of kids so I didn't try to get together with her."

"She has three young kids close in age. I guess they can be a handful sometimes."

"It sounded pretty chaotic over the phone. Anyway, she wasn't much help. Didn't know anything about Rosalind either. The only thing she could tell me was Rosalind has a brother. Do you know anything about him?"

"No, I never got very close with Rosalind. She was the kind of woman who kept to herself, at least when she wasn't flirting with the men. So it sounds as if this isn't going anywhere very fast," Leah said, disappointment in her voice.

"We're doing out best, Leah," Ty said. "We've had a lot to contend with along with Cliff's heart attack and the fire at GH."

"Oh, yes," she said, "please fill me in on that. I only saw one brief article about the fire and nothing since."

"Before we get to that we have something else to discuss," I said. "We went over to the TV station to see if we could talk to someone on the staff and were able to meet with the producer of the six o'clock news, Vanessa Anderson."

"What a good idea. I knew you two would be thorough."

"Have you ever heard of a fund-raising program called the X Factor?"

She looked at me with a scowl on her face. "Are you talking about the TV talent show?"

"No. It was a fund-raiser that Jeremy started some years ago."

"Why would he pick a crazy name like that?"

"This was before the talent show started here in the US. His fund-raiser was for histiocytosis X which is an autoimmune disease that usually affects children and is often fatal."

"Vanessa told us he said he started it because he had a young niece who suffered from the disease, yet she was unaware he even had a niece," Ty added.

"Have you asked Suzi Wallace about that?" Leah asked frowning. "Since she's Amy's sister surely she would know if there is such a niece and whether or not she suffers from this disease. He certainly never mentioned it to us, either the niece or the fund-raiser."

"Good idea," Ty said. "Hadn't occurred to us. Anyway Vanessa was sure Jeremy was pocketing the money. She reported it to the state attorney general's office, but Jeremy got in the wreck shortly afterward and went to jail and as far as she knows no one ever pursued it."

Leah shook her head sadly. "What a pitiful man he was. I don't know why Lawrence never saw through him. If only he hadn't hired him, all this probably wouldn't have happened. There are times when it doesn't pay to be softhearted."

"Lawrence must be a very good man," I said. "That's why we're trying hard to help him out. If we don't get sidetracked by any more extraneous things, we hope to make some progress."

"Okay, let's talk about those things. I'm really curious," Leah said.

And so we spent the next forty-five minutes or so describing Cliff's journey through the health care system and our journey through a major fire and disruption of life at GH.

"Wow. I see now you've really had your hands full. Sorry if I sounded testy on the phone but I was dwelling on Lawrence's problems while you two were just trying to keep your heads above water."

"Pretty much," I said.

Ty glanced at his watch. "Well, we don't want to keep you any longer. We'll try to do a better job of keeping in touch, maybe call you every few days."

"Please do. All I can do is just sit here and worry about everything. Since there's not much I can do, time weighs heavily on my hands."

On the way back to GH I said to Ty, "You know, we've been looking for Rosalind Voncannon. Maybe she's gone back to her maiden name. Have you thought of pursuing that?"

"I hadn't. Good call, Vi. I'll get right on it. And while I'm at it, I'll see if I can find a niece for Jeremy. Do you remember if it mentioned one in his obituary? Had there actually been a niece it surely would have mentioned her."

"I don't remember, Ty. Since I wasn't especially looking for one I could have skipped right over it."

When we got home I called Suzi Wallace.

"It's Vi Weatherspoon. Remember me?" I asked. "I talked to you a while back about your brother-in-law."

"Sure. What can I do for you?"

"Did Jeremy have any nieces?"

"No, why do you ask?"

"I was just tracking down some information on the family."

"That's it? That's all you want to know?"

"Yes. I heard he might have a niece."

"Well he doesn't. Is this important?"

"I don't think so. I'm only trying to gather whatever information I can about him. The more I know the better. Anyway thanks for your help."

Why tell her what I'd heard about The X Factor when her sister might be living off the proceeds. I didn't want to cause a rift.

That evening we had lasagna and salad for dinner. It was okay, but we were so used to having many choices for each meal that we were spoiled. It was eat what was offered or go hungry. I was beginning to wish that Greta would invite us to supper again.

"I talked to Suzi Wallace," I told Ty. "She told me Jeremy had no nieces."

"I came to the same conclusion. Pulled up the obituary and no mention there of any nieces or nephews. As far as I can figure out from records he was an only child."

"Honest to god, I can't imagine how he had the nerve to set up that charity and prey on people's sympathy. I hope no one gave him a large sum of money. But if they did and found out it was a scam that certainly could be a motive."

"That's possible. But it's been several years since it closed down. Would they wait this long to retaliate?"

"I don't know. Maybe they have a slow boiling point."

We were almost finished when I felt a tap on my shoulder and turned around to see Cora Lee.

"Oh, hi," I said wondering what she was after now.

"Just thought I'd share a little news I heard," she said with a smug look.

Since we were sitting at a table with several other people, I said, "We're ready to go. Why don't we step out into the hallway. Let someone else have our seats." I knew she would spread whatever malicious gossip she had around anyway, but I didn't want to be involved when she did.

I looked at Ty and he rolled his eyes at me as we stood

up to leave. But we felt as though we had no choice but to trail her out of the room like two obedient puppies.

Once in the hallway it was clear she couldn't wait to share her information. "I just heard they are going to charge Arthur Tisdale with setting the fire."

"How do you know that?" Ty asked.

"Oh, I have my sources," she said with a superior air.

"Do you know anything about his condition? Are they going to let him out of the hospital?" I asked.

"I understand he's improving, out of the woods so to speak. But I think he'll be in the hospital for a while yet."

"Well, that's kind of sad, isn't it?" I said. I didn't want her to think I appreciated the fact she couldn't wait to spread news, good or bad, around, but what do you say to someone like that?

Instead of parting to go to our separate wings, Ty grabbed my arm and led me toward the café.

"You want to drink coffee this time of the evening?" I asked. Both of us have our sleep issues and usually don't drink caffeine after twelve noon.

"No. Just had some thoughts I'd like to discuss."

We sat down at a corner table out of the way of any traffic in or out of the room.

"So?" I asked.

"I just had a hunch that Cora Lee's information was going to compel you to getting involved with Arthur. I want to suggest you leave it alone."

"Why?"

"Because we have our hands full with Lawrence and Deborah. Because they probably have pretty strong evidence against him. Because he's in the hospital and you can't get to him."

I'd never tell Ty this, but I'd been thinking pretty much the same thing. The fact that he was trying to talk me out of it though was the impetus to turn me around and make me want to get involved. I guess I can act like a petulant little kid when someone tries to lead me by the nose, but he'd better learn fast that it is the wrong approach with me. I decided if I did get engaged in any kind of investigation I wouldn't share it with him. I just shrugged. "One thing at a time I guess."

He patted my hand. "Good girl."

I was glad the light was dim in the café because I could feel the heat rise in my face. I had all sorts of ungracious comments swirling in my mind, but I bit my tongue and gave him a tight-lipped grimace hoping he'd take it for a smile. I rose thinking I needed to get out of there before I said something I'd regret. "Gotta go, Ty."

He looked a little startled, but probably thought I was anxious to watch a TV program.

TWENTY

I DID TURN on the TV and sat in front of it with Sweetie in my lap. She was even needier since her adventure in the woods. Every time I sat down she'd jump up, knead my legs with her paws, make a few turns and settle down for the duration.

I had no idea what program was on because my mind was on Arthur Tisdale. According to Cora Lee they were going to arrest him. Somehow I couldn't imagine any of our residents endangering the lives of everyone else because they didn't like the way the food was cooked. I know people do crazy things for seemingly minor reasons, but that was really beyond the pale. Maybe my faith in humanity was misplaced, but I knew I would love to hear his side of the story. However, if they wouldn't allow visitors, how was I going to do that?

And then an idea occurred to me. Possibly the conversation about Jeremy's relatives triggered it. Did Arthur have any sisters? What if I could pass myself off as an out-of-town sister coming to visit her gravely injured brother? Surely they would let me in. I knew I'd better find out first if he actually had one because next-of-kin would no doubt be on his records. It could be very embarrassing to say he was my brother only to find out no sister existed.

As much as I loathed doing it I called Cora Lee. If anyone knew about his background it would be our resident busybody.

"Hi Cora," I said when she answered. "I got to thinking

about what you told us this evening. Even though I don't know Arthur, he is a fellow resident, and I'm feeling quite sorry for him. I was wondering if he had any relatives who might come to his aid or is he's all alone?"

"Why? Are you planning on looking into the fire?"

This was my worst fear. "Oh, no, not at all. They probably have airtight evidence against him, and anyway I don't want to get involved on that end. I just thought if he had any relatives who were coming from out-of-town I could show them a little hospitality. Let them know the residents of Glendon Hills care."

"You really are softhearted, aren't you?" She made it sound like that was some kind of character defect.

"Maybe soft-*headed* is more like it. But I feel GH has a reputation to uphold of being a supportive community."

"Whatever. Yes, I've eaten here with Arthur a few times. He has two sisters, one in California and one in Idaho. I think they are both older and not well enough to travel, so I feel sure they won't come to be with him."

"Oh, that's a shame. Well, I suppose our staff is doing whatever they can to support him."

"Well, since he caused so much damage here I don't know how supportive they are feeling. In fact, if it were me, I'd sue the pants off of him."

I felt sure she would. "Thanks anyway for your help, Cora Lee. I know I can always count on you for information." I said it so it would sound like a compliment although I didn't mean it that way.

"Any time," she replied sounding pleased.

TY AND I met in the exercise room at ten the next morning and went through our paces. He told me he'd spent a couple of hours on the computer the night before looking for more information.

"I made a little progress last night. I found a record of Rosalind's marriage certificate. Her maiden name was Bainbridge."

"Fantastic! That should help."

"You'd think so. But I haven't been able to track down a Rosalind Bainbridge, so maybe she didn't go back to her maiden name. It's like she disappeared off the face of the earth."

"Not even a Facebook account?"

"She does have one. But nothing's been posted since she left the advertising agency. It's pretty obvious she doesn't want to be found."

"You gotta admit that sounds suspicious."

"Yes, that's true. But it doesn't necessarily mean she's guilty of murder. It could have something to do with a love affair gone wrong or all sorts of other things."

"I suppose so. But she's not off the hook in my mind."

"Mine either."

It seemed as though the more we found out, the less we could put it all together.

We had left the treadmills and made the rounds of the weight machines. We were lucky again to have the room to ourselves. I found that many people like to work out just before dinner so while we can have it to ourselves in the morning, it is usually pretty crowded in the late afternoon.

As we each shifted to the next piece of equipment that lined two walls of the room. I realized I was able to do more cycles on each one than I could the week before. Maybe I really was getting into better shape. Ty was busy pumping his arms up and down. He could even develop a little bicep to brag on if he continued. I decided we ought to consider continuing our workouts here even after our regular exercise class resumed.

After lunch Ty went to play with the Bridge Dudes. I

knew he'd be tied up all afternoon so I could drive to the hospital and try to get in to see Arthur Tisdale. Ty would never be the wiser.

Since it was another scorching day I dressed in knee-length shorts, which I knew were not flattering, and a sleeveless plaid blouse that exposed my flabby upper arms. But I decided that comfort outweighed fashion. Not that I ever dress in high style, but I normally wear long pants and sleeves that are at least below the elbow in deference to sagging flesh. However, when the sun beats down like it did that day, all my constraints are dropped in favor of ease.

I was just as glad to be in my car; I knew if Ty were driving his convertible he'd want to have the top down even if it was near a hundred degrees. Only rainstorms and temperatures below forty would force him to put up the top. Like it made sense to drive around with the top down and the heater on high.

I found my way to the burn unit when I got to the hospital. I stopped at the nurses' station and asked to see Arthur Tisdale.

"Only family is allowed to see him," an officious nurse said without even looking up at me. She was writing in a chart and obviously didn't want to be bothered.

"I'm his sister," I said.

She looked up startled. "I thought all his family lived out west somewhere."

"That's right, Idaho. I had some health problems and couldn't get here earlier, but I'm anxious to see him now."

She eyed me with suspicion. Oh boy, I thought, I'm in trouble now. But finally she pointed down the hall. "Room 618."

The room was at the end of a long hall. When I got to the door I saw a man, his eyes closed, with his arms totally wrapped in gauze and elevated on top of pillows. I knocked softly on the door as I entered hoping he was only resting and not deeply asleep.

He opened his eyes and stared at me. I judged him to be a bit younger than me, around seventy perhaps. His hair was dark brown but I could see a touch of gray at the roots which indicated to me he was a little vain. His face was square with shaggy eyebrows and a bulbous nose, his appearance reinforcing his pugnacious reputation.

"What now?" he asked. His demeanor was grumpy but I reasoned I too would be grumpy in his place. An air of resignation hung over him as if he was expecting the worst, whatever it might be.

I came close to his bed and spoke softly so I wouldn't be overheard in the hall.

"I'm Viola Weatherspoon from Glendon Hills."

"Well it's about time someone from that place came to see me. I feel like I've been hung out to dry." He frowned as he hit the remote to lift the head of the bed.

"May I pull up a chair?" I asked gesturing to a straight chair against the wall.

"Be my guest." He said without a hint of graciousness in his voice.

I hauled the chair over next to his bed and sat down.

"Look, as far as the nurses are concerned, I'm your sister from Idaho. They won't allow anyone but relatives visit you."

He looked at me with a scowl for a moment. "Okay. I'll call you Marcy just in case anyone asks. That's the name on the records. Now what's all this subterfuge about?"

"I'll be honest with you Arthur. The rumors have been flying ever since the fire and they're all about you. Everyone's convinced you set it."

"You didn't say. Are you from the administration or are you a resident?"

"I'm a resident. Administration wouldn't dare lie like I have to get in here. It could get them in a world of trouble."

"So why would you care about me? I don't think I've even met you."

"I'm sorry about that. I should have sought you out and introduced myself. But I would like to hear your side of the story. I know how rumors can be."

He looked at me silently for a moment gauging whether I was honest about my intentions or not. I guess he finally decided he had nothing to lose. "It's not just the residents who believe I did it. I'm going to be charged by the police with setting it as soon as I get out of here."

I decided not to be coy about why I was here. "So did you set it?"

"Well, you don't beat about the bush do you?"

"No. I'm not here to play games with you."

"So why do you want to know?" His eyes challenged me. It was obvious he was not a trusting soul.

"I just have a feeling that you had nothing to do with it. I've heard about how you've complained about the meals since you moved to Glendon Hills. But that doesn't mean you'd do anything as horrific as that."

He gave me a bitter smile. "That's quite an assumption to make since you don't know me at all."

"I suppose it is. But there you have it." I shrugged. Somewhere along the line this man had learned to trust no one. I wondered if I'd ever find out why.

He was silent for a moment. Then he said, "Of course I didn't set it. I may be hardheaded, but I'd never endanger anyone's life. I was a chef for years in Cleveland at a top rated restaurant, and I guess my expectations were unreal when I moved to Glendon Hills. I thought the menu was boring, and the execution left a lot to be desired. Crazy me, I thought by getting on their case I could raise the level of the preparation and it would benefit everyone."

"Well, most of us are pleased with the food there," I said. "Mostly we're happy that we no longer have to cook since lots of us don't like to."

"The problem is you don't have a discriminating palate. You don't know what good food should taste like." The tone of superiority in his voice was off-putting. No wonder people disliked him.

"Discriminating or not, let's get to the point here. Why are you being charged if you had nothing to do with it?"

He sighed deeply. "Long story. Sure you want to hear it?"

"Of course I do. That's why I'm here."

He squirmed a little and then settled down. "I'm so tired of lying in this bed I could scream. Everything starts to hurt after a while. Anyway, back to my story. I exercise every evening by walking the halls for thirty minutes or so. By eight-thirty everyone is usually in their apartment or downstairs in the multi-purpose room if there's a program. I don't especially like to interact with people if I don't have to so that's a good time for me."

That's kind of sad I thought, but I wasn't going to judge him for being antisocial. "Go on," I said.

"As I walked by the dining room I could smell smoke. I looked in and saw it was coming from under the kitchen door. So I went in there and saw a waste container full of paper in flames."

"And then what? Did you try to put it out?"

"It was one of those big ones," he said stretching out his bandaged arms far apart to indicate its size, "and the flames were shooting maybe eight feet in the air. It was close to the new flambé cart."

"What's that?"

"They just bought it. It's a cart on wheels that has a propane two-burner cook top and you can use it tableside or at a buffet to cook over an open flame. They were planning on using it at the next party. It adds a bit of flamboyance to special occasions."

"See?" I said. "We're not such hicks down here if we have something like that."

He gave me a look of pity and shook his head. "Anyway, there were some big bottles of rum next to it. That's what you use to make bananas foster and it's highly flammable. I knew once the fire reached those, everything would explode in flame. I felt I had to get them out of there."

"Weren't you afraid? I'd freak out!" I exclaimed envisioning the whole of Glendon Hills in flames.

"I guess I didn't have time to think about it. I grabbed the bottles, but when I did the fire flared out from the waste can and burned my arms. It was a miracle the rum didn't explode. I held them to my chest and ran out through the dining room into the hall. One of the security guards was running toward the kitchen, the alarm was sounding all over the building by then, and I almost collided with him. He grabbed my arm and snatched the bottles away. When he realized I'd been burned, he sat me down in a chair in the lobby and told me to stay put. He ran off down the hall with the rum and I suppose he was putting it away some place to use later as evidence. In a few minutes he was back just as the fire department and everyone else descended upon the building."

"So you just sat there while they fought the fire?"

"No, Jake, the security guy, summoned the paramedics who took care of me. Not only were my arms pretty badly burned, but I had smoke inhalation too. I'm still having inhalation therapy."

"Wow," I said, "that's quite a story. So you're saying that you're being charged with setting the fire because you were trying to get rid of the bottles of rum."

He shrugged. "What else could it be?"

"Did you explain to the police or fire marshal or whoever what happened?"

"Of course. But they don't believe me."

I looked at him long and hard. It felt as though he was telling the truth but he could have been a very accomplished liar. "Could that have anything to do with the fact that you threatened to burn down the place?"

His brow knitted and he looked confused at first and then furious. "Who told you that?"

I wouldn't normally have mentioned any names. But Cora Lee had spread the word all over GH so everyone knew who was saying it. "Our favorite gossip, Cora Lee."

He closed his eyes and shook his head. "That woman is beyond belief. What I actually said was *someone's* going to burn this place down some day. And what I meant was the kitchen staff is so incompetent *they'll* probably burn it down."

That sounded just enough like Cora Lee that I almost believed him. I knew she could take words and twist them around to suit her. Could it be that she was hard of hearing and misunderstood? Or was she mean-spirited enough she enjoyed misquoting people to suit her purposes? And if that were true why would she want to hurt Arthur? Arson is a very serious charge.

TWENTY-ONE

IN SPITE OF the fact that he wasn't the most pleasant person, Arthur's story had the ring of truth about it. Maybe I'm just a sucker for sob stories, but after all the years of working with all ages at the Girl Scouts I feel I have a pretty good built-in bullshit detector. I thought it would be a crying shame if he ended up in jail for trying to save Glendon Hills and its residents. It seemed to me that it was worth looking into. Apparently no one else was on his side. I wondered if Administration would step forward if he was charged when he got out of the hospital or if they, too, were convinced he was guilty. This was going to be a very sticky situation though. How could I look into it without Ty finding out? Would it take away from our attempt to help Lawrence and Debbie? I had a lot to think about. I didn't feel I was in a position at the moment to make any guarantees.

"Well, I'm glad I got to hear your side of the story," I told him.

"But do you believe me?" It was definitely a plea. I suppose he felt I was the only hope he had.

I gathered up my purse, set the chair back against the wall, and as I turned to leave said, "I do, Arthur. I hope things work out for you." It was a lame answer, but I wasn't going to promise I would help him because I wasn't sure I could.

I inquired at the nursing station whether a therapist by the name of Bainbridge worked there, and, after they consulted their computer, was told there was an occupational therapist on the orthopedic floor which was one floor down. Hallelujah!

I checked at the nurses' station on the fifth floor and was told Ted was in room 529 with a patient but I could wait for him in the hall.

I hurried down the corridor and caught him just as he was exiting the room. His name tag assured me it was Ted Bainbridge.

"Ted," I said breathlessly, catching his arm. "Could I talk to you for just a minute, please?"

I emphasized the "please" to convey the urgency I felt.

He looked a bit startled then glanced at his watch. "I'm running a bit late but I guess I could give you five minutes or so."

I gestured toward the waiting room. "Can we go there for a minute? There's something important I want to talk to you about."

He scowled but followed me reluctantly back down the hall and sat down beside me in a row of chairs.

"What is it?" he asked.

"Are you by any chance Rosalind Voncannon's brother?" No sense in wasting time on small talk.

He looked startled. "How do you know Roz?"

"I live in Idaho now but I'm here visiting my brother who's upstairs in the burn unit. I used to live in Guilford City and have a friend here who was close to your sister. She's been trying to get in touch with Roz but it seems like she's disappeared into thin air." I'd decided to maintain the fake identity I'd given the nurses on the burn unit. I knew if he had any idea why I was looking for her, he would clam up immediately. So I added, "They were very close and she's so worried that something has happened to her." I prayed he wouldn't ask me who my friend was.

He chewed on his bottom lip while he considered my question. Finally he said, "Roz has gone through something of a bad patch. She wanted to get away from Guilford City and put it behind her. I'm not sure she wants to be found."

How was I going to get around this? I thought of an approach and hoped I'd be forgiven for another lie in the pursuit of the greater good. "This friend worked with Roz and after your sister left heard that Roz was due for some back pay but the company couldn't find her to send it to her. She thought she might need this extra money. It was a pretty nice amount."

He nodded his head. "Yeah. I've tried to help her a little but I don't make all that much. She definitely could use it. Do you know how much it is?"

"I have no idea."

"How about if your friend gives the money to me and I'll send it to her?"

I screwed up my face as if I were thinking hard about it. "I don't know. She might not feel that trusting. Why not give her the address so she can send it directly?"

"I don't think my sister would want me to give that out."

"How about her phone number so my friend can talk to her and they can work out an arrangement?" I was desperate to get anything I could.

"I guess I could do that. Have you got something to write on?"

I picked up my pocketbook from the floor and rifled through it till I came upon a small notepad I carry around and a pen and wrote down the number.

"I'm running late," he said as he got up. "Gotta go."

"Thanks," I called after him as he hurried down the hall.

Well, now I had Roz's number but I wasn't sure how helpful it would be. I couldn't exactly call her up and ask if she'd killed Jeremy. And I doubted I could track her down in the age of the cell phone. To get so close and yet be so far away from finding her.

As I drove back to GH I wondered how I was going to share Roz's phone number with Ty without telling him what I'd been doing at the hospital. And then I thought what the heck? Ty isn't my keeper. I'm a free senior citizen and I can do whatever I want to do without having to justify it to anyone else. It was very liberating.

We met for dinner at the prescribed time. We managed to find two seats in an isolated corner which freed us to discuss whatever we liked.

"So how did the bridge go?" I asked.

"Terrible. I had lousy hands all afternoon. It seems I've had bad hands all month as a matter of fact."

"Why do you continue to play then?"

I could almost hear his thoughts: *What a dumb question.* "Because it's fun. Why else?"

"It doesn't sound like fun."

"You just don't understand."

"I guess not."

"What did you do all afternoon?"

And so came the moment of truth. "I went to the hospital to see Arthur Tisdale."

"What?" He frowned. "I understood we weren't getting involved with him."

"I believe *you* decided that. I thought about it and figured he needed some kind of a friend. I'd hate to be in the hospital and not have anyone visit me."

"But don't they only allow family?"

I grinned at him. "I was Marcy, his sister from Idaho."

Ty rolled his eyes. "Jeez, Vi. Weren't you taking a risk? How did you know her name and where she was from? Or did you make that up out of whole cloth?"

"As to taking a risk what were they going to do if they found out I was lying? Throw me out? Call the cops? I don't think they could have done much."

Ty was wrapping his spaghetti around his fork like an expert. I always admired that. I cut mine up in short pieces so I don't make a fool of myself. Once he got it wound up he stopped and said, "How did you know he even had a sister?"

"Who is the font of all knowledge around here?" I took a bite of garlic bread and watched his face as it dawned on him.

"You asked Cora Lee?" It was as if he were asking if I went to the devil himself.

"Yup. She knew he had two sisters, their names, and where they lived. That was all I needed to know."

He finally ate the forkful of spaghetti and then settled back with a sigh. "So how is Arthur? As cantankerous as ever? Bitching about the hospital food?"

"Remarkably we never discussed the food there. He was upset that no one from GH has gone to see him."

"Did you explain only family is allowed?"

"I did. I'm not sure he knew that. Anyway, I was able to get his side of the story."

"Which is not necessarily the truth."

"I know, Ty. But somehow it sounded right to me."

He gave me a slow smile. "Is this woman's intuition?"

I shrugged. "Call it what you like, I guess I believed him."

"Okay. Tell me what Arthur had to say. I'll reserve judgment for now."

And so I launched into the story of how he ran into the kitchen when he saw the smoke coming from under the door, saw the bottles of rum and knew he had to save Glendon Hills by getting it away from the fire. "And his

arms were burned pretty badly when he did that. I'd say
he's something of a hero."

"Providing his story is true."

TWENTY-TWO

"YOU'RE AN OLD curmudgeon yourself, Ty."

"No I'm not. Just a skeptic. Why wouldn't the cops believe him then?"

"Oh, that. One of our security guys ran into him as he left the kitchen. He grabbed the rum out of his hands and took it somewhere, Arthur thinks to hold as evidence. He sat Arthur down in the lobby and summoned the medics."

"Well, that would look pretty suspicious."

"I suppose so. But I believed him."

"What about the fact he threatened to burn the place down?"

"He claims he said *someone* will burn it down and he meant incompetent staff. Cora Lee misquoted him. Can't you see how they've twisted everything around?"

"I'll still reserve judgment, thank you."

I stuck out my tongue at him.

"Honestly Vi. Is that the way you ran the Girl Scouts?"

I put on my best snobbish look and peered down my nose at him while holding a pretend lorgnette. "I conducted myself with great dignity I'll have you know."

That broke him up. He laughed so hard he dropped spaghetti in his lap. "Look what you made me do."

"Come on," I said rising from my chair. "Let's take our cookies and walk around the grounds. It seems to have cooled off a bit."

Still chuckling, he picked up the errant strands of spaghetti with his paper napkin, rolled it up and put it on his plate. "Good thing I wore washable workout pants, Let me have your napkin."

I handed it to him and he stuck it in his glass of water and rubbed the reddish spot the sauce had left. "Most of it came out. I hope no one thinks I stabbed myself."

"No one's going to notice. Besides they don't have vivid imaginations like you do," I said.

We walked out the back door onto the concrete pathway that circumvents the building. It still was quite warm but a soft breeze had come up which made it bearable. The woods were full of sounds of buzzing insects and snapping twigs as squirrels frolicked from limb to limb and other invisible creatures roamed the deepening shadows under the lush canopy of leaves. The song birds added a touch of melody to it all. It was beautiful out here and once again I thanked the powers-that-be that I lived in such a delightful place with wonderful friends and neighbors.

We walked silently for a few minutes. I think Ty, too, was experiencing a feeling of gratitude for having found Glendon Hills. Even though we grumbled occasionally over this minor rule or that insignificant irritation like our current meal arrangement, we both felt that we couldn't have made a better choice.

I almost hated to break the spell by talking about Roz Voncannon, but I felt it important to share what I'd learned.

"Let's sit over there on that bench and eat our cookies," I said. Before we sat down we read the inscription on the brass plaque and realized it was the bench dedicated to Ginger's parrot Lester. That seemed appropriate because we were going to talk about our present investigation. Lester had been involved in our first one.

"I found out something else, Ty. I was so excited to think I had a lead, but I'm not sure it's going to be all that helpful."

"Are we talking about Arthur?"

"No, we're talking about Roz Voncannon."

"I'm confused. How did we get on that subject?"

Just then one of the residents approached us walking her dog. The perimeter path is very popular with the dog people. It's lined with waste stations where they can get bags to scoop the poop to dispose of it.

We greeted her as she passed us and munched on our cookies till she was out of earshot before continuing.

"Okay," said Ty. "What's this about Roz?"

"Do you remember that Deborah told me she had a brother who worked in a local hospital?"

He thought for a minute. "Not really."

"Well, Candy first mentioned him but didn't know anything about him. Then I called Deborah and found out about the hospital. But we knew his name wouldn't be Voncannon because Roz had been married."

"Oh yeah. The light is beginning to dawn."

"Then you found out her maiden name is Bainbridge."

Ty grinned widely. Pointing his finger at my chest he said, "And I'll bet you found someone named Bainbridge at the hospital today."

"Bingo!" I said. "In fact he's an occupational therapist."

"How about that!" Ty by now had forgotten he was upset with me for visiting Arthur. "Did you find out where Roz is?"

I lost my grin. I knew this was going to be disappointing. "I'm afraid not. He said she was going through a bad patch and needed to get away from Guilford City. So I made up a cockamamie story about how a friend of hers found out she had back pay coming to her but couldn't find her to pass it along."

"But he still wouldn't tell you where she was." He looked pretty crestfallen.

"I finally got her cell phone number, but I don't know how much help that is going to be."

"You're right. We know it's a new phone because the old one was no longer in service. Maybe it has a different area code which could narrow it down a bit, but still wouldn't be very helpful. But maybe we can figure out something we could do."

I stood up ready to continue our walk. "Let's forgot it for this evening. We can sleep on it and perhaps come up with an idea. But let's just enjoy this beautiful evening for now."

And so we walked the whole circumference of the building arriving back at the door of the community room where we started out. Only a few stragglers remained eating their dinner as we passed through and greeted them before parting in the hall to go to our separate wings.

Sweetie greeted me at my door as always. When I sat down to watch TV she jumped into my lap and purred contentedly.

"I can see why you were drawn to the great outdoors," I told her as I petted her. "It's so beautiful out there. But you're much safer here with me."

Her tail quivered just a bit as if to signal her agreement.

TWENTY-THREE

WHEN TY AND I met in the café the next morning, I asked, "So do you have any bright ideas about how to find Roz?"

"Well, yeah, I did come up with one idea."

"Great. That's one more than I have," I said and got up to refill my cup. When I sat down again I said, "Okay, let's hear it."

"You said you told Roz's brother that she had back pay coming to her. He's probably already called her and told her so she'll be primed. Why don't we enlist Lawrence to call and offer to send it to her? I'm sure she'd give him her address."

"I don't know why I didn't think of that. Then we can go to her house and question her."

Ty sat thoughtfully, his fingers tented in front of his mouth. Finally he said, "*If* she'll talk to us. We have to think of a way to ensure that she does."

"We could say Lawrence insisted she only get the money if she helps him out."

"In other words it's a blatant bribe and she'll know it."

We both sat in a funk wondering if this subterfuge could possibly work. Finally I said, "If she needs cash so badly and yet refuses to take the money, it would be an indication she's probably guilty of something. Don't you think?"

Ty nodded slowly. "I guess. Then at least we'll know where she is and perhaps could find out what she's been up to. Anyway, what other choice do we have?"

"None that I can think of."

So we agreed that I would contact Lawrence after we went through our exercises.

When I called an hour later, Deborah answered the phone.

"Vi! We keep hoping to hear from you. What's going on?"

A pang of guilt rushed through me and I realized I hadn't talked to her in some time. We hadn't been keeping them in the loop just as we'd failed to keep Leah up to date. There were too many people involved that needed to know what we were doing. When our attention is riveted on an investigation, we sometimes forget that those on the periphery are anxious to know what's happening.

"I guess it has been a while since we talked," I said sheepishly. "I wanted to ask a favor of Lawrence."

"We're both dying to see you and Ty. Could you come over and fill us in on what is going on?"

"Well, sure, we could do that."

"How about lunch today? Or do you have other plans?"

She certainly did seem anxious. "No, we're free." A lunch away from GH would be a treat. The caterers didn't have much imagination, and I was getting tired of the same things over and over.

"Twelve-thirty then?"

"Okay. Can I bring something?"

"No, no, just yourselves."

I called Ty and we planned to meet in the lobby at 12:10.

On the way to the Rinehart's he said, "I guess it has been a while since we've talked to them."

"True. But it's not like we've been sitting around twiddling our thumbs. We've been working for them the whole time."

"We just need to let them know that."

Lawrence and Deborah greeted us like we were long

lost relatives. She had set the dining table with her best china and a cut-glass crystal vase full of dark red roses as the centerpiece. It looked like we were having a party and maybe she thought of it that way. It only added to my guilty conscience.

"Let's go ahead and eat," Deborah said, "and we can talk over lunch."

She must have kept a well-stocked kitchen because in the couple of hours since I called her she put together a delicious chicken salad along with fresh sliced tomatoes and cucumbers and warm rolls.

As we ate we brought them up-to-date on Cliff's condition and the fire at GH.

"We knew about Cliff," Lawrence said. "His office called us when he had the heart attack. And of course that has worried us a lot because we don't know who is working on our case if anyone at all."

"I'm sure they have someone on it," Ty said. "If Cliff had his way, he'd be at the office working full time. But Greta is making sure he takes it easy for at least six weeks."

"We certainly wouldn't want him to endanger his health," Deborah said, "though it still makes us nervous. But, guys, we didn't know about your fire. Somehow we missed that piece of news. How are you coping?"

"A caterer is bringing our meals and serving them in the community room. That's where we normally do our exercises."

"So you not only can't exercise, but you're probably eating high-calorie food. Am I right?" Lawrence asked.

Ty laughed. "Spaghetti, lasagna, meat loaf—I guess you know the drill. But Vi and I are working out in the weight room to make up for it."

"Do you know how the fire started?" Deborah asked.

Ty looked at me and I looked at him. Finally I said,

"That's under debate right now. Some people think a resident started it, but I don't.'"

"Vi, the champion of the underdog," Ty said as he raised his glass of tea as a toast.

"That's because she has a heart of gold," Deborah countered.

She got up to clear the table and Lawrence said, "You said something about needing a favor when you called."

"Let's wait until Deborah's finished clearing the table. I want her to hear it too." I said.

She brought us key lime pie for dessert and coffee to go with it.

"Okay, now," Lawrence said. "Tell us what you want us to do."

I began. "If you'll remember we've been unable to locate Roz Voncannon, and it seems suspicious that she has cut all ties. I talked to her coworkers, and the only thing I learned was she had a brother. And you, Deborah, told me her brother worked at a hospital here. Didn't know his name or which hospital."

"Don't tell me you found him," Lawrence interrupted.

"With Ty's help I did. Ty found out Roz's maiden name was Bainbridge. Then I decided to visit the GH resident who got burned in the fire. While I was there I inquired about a therapist named Bainbridge and learned he is an occupational therapist there."

"Wow," Deborah said, "good for you."

"I felt sure he was probably her brother, and I was desperate to learn her address. So I waylaid him outside the room and told him this big fib. I didn't know what else to do."

"And what big fib is that?" Lawrence asked. He had a gleam in his eye that told me he loved the idea of subterfuge.

"I don't know if you'll appreciate this or not, but I told

him you discovered Roz had some back pay coming and you needed her address to send it to her."

Deborah clapped. "Brilliant!"

I shrugged. "Well, it seemed so at the time only he refused to give it to me."

She looked so crestfallen I wanted to go over and put my arms around her. "But all is not lost," I said. "I finally wheedled her phone number out of him. Of course that isn't much help since it's a cell phone. I'll let Ty tell you what we propose."

"We thought you, Lawrence, could call her and tell her you want to get the money to her. You don't have to say you'll *mail* it, but she'll probably think that's what will happen. Once you get her address Vi and I will go talk to her."

"Do you think you can get her to talk?" Lawrence asked.

"If we tell her she won't get any money unless she does."

"In other words you'll bribe her."

"That's exactly what I said when Vi suggested it. But sometimes you have to go with underhanded methods even if you don't like it much."

"It works for me," Lawrence said. "I already offered you money for your library to help us out. I'm ready to give more if it will help exonerate us."

"We can't promise that," I said. "It might lead nowhere at all. But, honestly, we are running out of ideas."

"Our money isn't going to do us a bit of good if we're sitting in jail. I think it's a good investment," Deborah chimed in.

"So how much do you want me to offer her?" Lawrence asked.

'We don't know Roz at all. Maybe you know her well enough to gauge how much would entice her to talk."

Lawrence thought about it for a few minutes. "I don't

want it to be too low so she can easily dismiss it. How about five thousand?"

"That's extremely generous," Ty said. "You sure you want to spend that much?"

"I'd spend much more if I had to. Let's give that a try."

We gave the phone number to Lawrence before returning to GH. He was going to try and reach her immediately and let us know as soon as he had an address. "If she lives out of town, I'll cover any expenses you have driving to see her," he told us as we left.

"Maybe we'll get a little trip out of this," Ty said on our way home.

"At someone else's expense. I like that part," I said.

We heard nothing from Lawrence the rest of the day. I prayed the phone number was good and she hadn't discontinued that service as well.

A gospel choir gave a concert in the multi-purpose room that evening. It seemed the perfect antidote to sitting around wondering if Lawrence was ever going to call. As I listened to them sing familiar old hymns I never once thought about the Rineharts or Arthur Tisdale or the burned-out kitchen or anything else that was worrying me.

TWENTY-FOUR

THE NEXT MORNING in the café, reality had settled back in and Ty and I tried to figure out why Lawrence had not called us.

"If her phone service has been discontinued surely he would let us know," Ty said.

"She might be leery of answering it when she sees his name on the caller I.D. screen," I said. "If she left under such unhappy circumstances, she'd probably wonder why he wanted to talk to her."

"Maybe she went somewhere without her phone."

"Now how often does that happen?" I asked. "Don't want to be negative, Ty, but take away a young person's phone it's like cutting off a hand or a foot. They can't live without them."

He sipped his coffee. "You're right. It's an appendage."

"Where do we go from here if he can't get in touch?"

He rubbed his chin dejectedly. "Hell if I know."

We went about our exercises without enthusiasm. Neither of us had much to say as we each wallowed in our feelings of frustration. It seemed we'd spent a lot of time and effort trying to help the Rineharts without any visible results.

When we were done Ty said, "I need to go to the grocery store for a few things. Want to come along?"

"No thanks," I said. "I've got plenty of food right now. Besides it's supposed to be in the nineties today and I'd just as soon stay here where it's cool."

What I didn't say was that his trunk was so small in his little convertible that chances were we couldn't get more than a sack or two of groceries apiece in it.

When he left to get his car keys from his apartment, I started to go back to mine, but had an idea and walked toward the area of administrative offices instead. I wanted to talk to Frank Kaufman, the Director of Operations.

His door was open and he was working on his computer. I knocked lightly on the open door and he turned and smiled.

"Come in, come in, Ms. Weatherspoon," he said, gesturing to the chair in front of his desk. One of the things I like best about GH is that everyone in administration is so willing to talk with you and try to solve any problems. "How can I help you?" he asked.

"I wanted to ask you about the fire in the kitchen," I said.

"What is it you want to know?"

"Is it definite they are going to charge Arthur Tisdale with setting it?"

His smile disappeared. "I'm sorry, but I can't discuss this with you."

"Well, I think you should know I visited Arthur in the hospital. He says he was carrying the rum bottles out of the kitchen to prevent them from exploding and making it worse. It seems to me he's a hero. The fire could have been catastrophic had they gone up."

Frank looked stricken. "Look, Ms. Weatherspoon, this is in the hands of the fire marshal and the police. I can't comment on it. I'm sorry, but that's the way it is."

I knew I was being dismissed. I didn't blame Frank. Rules are rules. But it made me even more frustrated.

When I left to go back to my apartment I saw Nichole Bardy at the front desk picking up a package. Nichole is in charge of the dining room and was now working with the caterer to provide the meals in the community room. I approached her and asked, "Have you got a minute, Nichole?"

She looked at her watch. "I've got about ten minutes before I need to start setting up for lunch."

We settled onto the sofa in the reception area, and I got straight to the point. "Nichole, was anyone on the kitchen staff fired just before the kitchen fire?"

Her eyes widened. "Why are you asking, Viola?"

"I saw Arthur Tisdale in the hospital, and he swears he didn't start it. He says he saw the bottles of rum next to the flambé cart and grabbed them up and ran before they blew up. Now he's being charged with setting it."

Nichole began chewing on a fingernail. I could tell she was nervous discussing this. "But I heard he made threats."

"Look," I said, "one of our residents, I won't name names, is quite the gossip. She took something he said, mostly in jest, and twisted it around. He never threatened to do anything."

"Well, he has certainly been a thorn in our side. He complained about everything. Just because he was a big-time chef didn't mean he could run the show here."

I put my hand on top of hers. I could tell she was upset over Arthur's constant criticism. I'd feel the same way in her shoes. "But that doesn't mean he would do something that would threaten the lives of the people who live here. I can tell you I really believed him."

She let out a deep sigh. "You won't tell anyone I told you this, will you?"

"Of course not."

"We did let one of the busboys go about a week before the fire. He was constantly late getting here and then was caught smoking in the men's room. This is a no smoking campus and that won't be tolerated."

"Can you give me his name?"

She didn't speak for a couple of minutes. "I don't want to get in trouble over this."

"No one will know that you told me. I'm sure I could get the information from any of the servers." Maybe or maybe not.

"It was Billy Bates. He's a student at Cornwallis University. I know he was awfully upset because he said he needed the money for tuition. I told him he shouldn't have broken the rules then."

I grabbed both of her hands and squeezed them. "Thank you, Nichole. Maybe, just maybe, you've saved an innocent man from being prosecuted."

"You think you can get Billy to confess? That is if he really is guilty," she amended, not quite sure I was on the right track.

"If not, at least I could give his name to the police to investigate. Did they ever ask you about anyone being fired?"

"No. I guess they were sure it was Arthur. And for that matter so was I."

"Well, maybe we can turn this around. I'm at least going to give it a try."

Nichole stood up. "I've got to get downstairs. I hope I helped you."

"I'm pretty sure you did."

Ty was back from the store in time for lunch.

"Man, it's hot out there," he said as we stood line for our soup and sandwiches.

"Did you put up the top and turn on the air conditioning?"

"Heck no. If I did that I might as well have bought a coupe."

I just smiled and shook my head. Sometimes there's just no reasoning with men.

Once we were at a table I told him about my morning's interviews.

"So you think this kid Billy might have started it?"

"Well, I'm convinced Arthur didn't."

"And so what do you propose we do?"

"Talk to him."

"And you think he's just going to break down and confess?"

I sipped some soup as I thought about that. I had imagined he'd want to get it off his conscience. But I was probably dreaming. "Mmmm, it would be the best case scenario, wouldn't it?"

"But unrealistic perhaps?"

When he asked me that point blank, I had to admit to myself that it was. "Any suggestions?"

"I think we should try and find out where Billy lives and if he has a roommate," Ty said.

"What's a roommate got to do with anything?"

"Well, you know how guys like to brag. If he did start the fire, he probably couldn't resist telling someone about it."

"Most likely his roommate."

"That's what I was thinking."

I could see where he was going with this. "And we need to convince this kid that the wrong man was being prosecuted and would go to jail."

"And hope the roommate has a conscience and wants to make things right. It's worth a try," Ty said. "Of course this is all predicated on the idea Billy is guilty. Maybe he's pure as driven snow."

"Somehow I doubt it. Anyway it beats sitting around and twiddling our thumbs," I replied.

The next thing was to find out where Billy lived and if he roomed with someone. Ty said he'd see what he could do. Since no institution wants to give out information these days he knew it might be difficult.

Sure enough, he told me he came up empty when we met for dinner.

We were standing in line for the evening meal and I said, "I've got an idea."

Glendon Hills was using as many of the dining room staff as they could to dish up the food as we passed through the line. They could have set it up so we served ourselves, but I'm sure they wanted to keep as many of the staff employed as possible while the kitchen was being rebuilt. They were mostly young, many of them university students, and there seemed to be a lot of camaraderie between them. I had a hunch at least one of them would know how to contact Billy.

I told Ty this while we were eating our dinner. I knew I couldn't approach them while they were so busy, but suggested we come back at 7:30 when the last of the residents were eating and the staff would be cleaning up.

We played billiards in the first floor lounge during the forty-five minutes we had to wait for the dining room to clear. Ty had wanted to teach me for a long time, but I always had an excuse. This night I couldn't think of a solitary reason to get out of it so I reluctantly followed him to the lounge. I'd never touched a cue in my life and I was afraid of making a fool of myself. I would rather have played ping pong even though I was pretty bad at it, but the table had been in the community room and had been taken down when dining services were set up there.

He showed me how to hold the cue and hit the balls, and after a disastrous start, I actually started getting a few in the pockets. It was more fun than I wanted to admit.

Of course I wasn't going to become an expert in three-quarters of an hour, but I learned it could be more enjoyable than I'd imagined. I decided I'd be amenable to playing again.

At 7:30 we went back to find a server we could talk to. All the residents had gone, and they were cleaning up the buffet counter and bussing the tables.

I pointed out a young woman who was working at a table on the far side of the room. She's friendly and efficient and one of my favorites on the wait staff. "Let's talk to Caitlin," She was far enough away from other staff that no one would hear our conversation.

"Hi, Caitlin," I said as we approached. "How's it working out for you down here?"

"Hi, Ms. Weatherspoon, Mr. Landowski. Not too bad. I'd rather be upstairs, of course, but I'm just glad I have a job. They couldn't use everyone, you know."

"I feel bad about that. Hopefully the dining room will be open again soon and they can hire all the old staff back."

"If they haven't found other jobs," Caitlin said sadly. "We're like family and we miss those guys."

"I know you do. Everybody's anxious to get back to normal," Ty said.

"Caitlin, we want to ask a favor of you," I told her. "This is really important and we need this information. We'd be so appreciative if you can help us."

She set the stack of plates she was carrying down on the table and looked at us with a mixture of alarm and curiosity. "What kind of favor would that be?"

"Do you know where Billy Bates lives and how to get in touch with him?" Ty asked.

She scowled. "Could I get in trouble over this?"

"No, not at all," I reassured her. "We got his name from

someone in Administration. But we don't know where he lives and it's important we find him."

She looked from one to the other of us clearly not convinced.

"We know he's a student at Cornwallis University," Ty said. "Does he live on campus?"

Finally she seemed to relax and realize there was no reason for concern if she told us where he lived. All she could have known was he got fired for smoking on campus and that's not exactly a major crime. I doubted very much he would have told anyone on the GH staff if he started the fire.

"Can you tell me why you want to see him?" she asked.

We hadn't considered she'd ask us that question. I frantically tried to think of a believable answer when Ty said, "I'm sorry, Caitlin, it's a personal thing. I'm sure you understand."

I wanted to pat him on the back and say, "Good job!" He effectively shut off her questions and yet let her think it was urgent. She'd no doubt spend the rest of the day trying to figure out what "personal" reason we could possibly have.

She blushed a little as if embarrassed she'd asked. "I know he's in room 237 in Manning Hall. He left some personal items here and I took them over to him."

"Oh," I said brightly." If I remember right that's an old dorm where you have to share a room instead of having a single." I knew absolutely nothing about the campus or the dorm but hoped she didn't realize that. I wanted her to think I was only making small talk.

"You're right," she said. "Billy was pretty pissed off about that but you have to be a junior or senior to get a single."

Ty picked up on the conversation. "I remember the

roommate I had in college. What a jerk. I hope Billy had better luck."

"I think he gets along okay with Roberto. You know how it is when two guys have to share a small space," Caitlin said. "But mostly they just try to stay out of each other's hair."

"Well, we'll let you get back to work," I said. "Thanks Caitlin."

"Good job," Ty whispered in my ear as we left the community room.

TWENTY-FIVE

THE NEXT MORNING we still hadn't heard from Lawrence.

"Do you think we should call him and find out what's going on?" I asked.

"Not yet. He must still be trying to reach Roz or he would have let us know. This is so important to him he'll do everything he can to get in touch with her. Let's wait a day or two."

"Okay, then, what are we going to do about Billy?"

We were side by side on the treadmills and Ty had just raised his to create an uphill climb. I wondered if this was a challenge for me to keep up with him. I raised mine too, but not nearly as steep.

Ty was getting a little breathless. I was worried he'd overdo it. "We need to get up with...Roberto without Billy...knowing about it."

"And how do you propose we do that?"

"I laid in bed...and thought about it...last night. Didn't get much sleep...but I came up...with an idea." He spoke between little puffs of breath.

"For heaven's sake, Ty. Put that treadmill level before you have a heart attack. I don't need to have both men out of commission who mean the most to me."

He punched the button to lower it and said, "I didn't know you cared," with a shy smile.

I knew he was being ironic, he was the type who was

uncomfortable with any kind of praise, but I realized I'd never told him how much his friendship meant to me.

"Ty Landowski, you know you're the brother I never had. As nice as it is to live at Glendon Hills, having you as my friend has made it twice as nice."

I saw his ears go pink and he seemed unable to reply. Finally he said, "All I can say is ditto to you, Vi."

Now *I* was feeling embarrassed and ready to change the subject. "Okay, tell me what you dreamed up."

"I thought I'd call Administration at the university. Tell them I found a textbook with the names "Roberto" and "Manning" written in it. Ask them if there was a Roberto Manning enrolled as I'd like to return it. I feel sure they would figure out that Manning meant the dorm and give me his last name. Surely there aren't two Robertos living there."

"It's good he doesn't have a common name."

"That was a real stroke of luck."

I was ready to get off the treadmill and make my way around the weight machines. So I brought it to a stop and said, "So then what? If we go to their room won't Billy recognize us? Surely he would have some idea why we were there."

"No. I'll think up an excuse to contact Roberto and have him meet us somewhere. I plan to look up his Facebook page. That should give me some information I can use to entice him to see us." Ty slowed it down and stepped off the treadmill.

"Providing you can get access to it."

"Kids that age don't usually worry about strangers looking at their page. I'll bet I can."

"Let me see it too. Maybe I'll have an idea."

"Sure. Let's do our round of the machines and then go back to my apartment."

BACK IN TY'S apartment I waited while he called the Administration Department at Cornwallis University. It didn't take long for him to come up with the name of Alvarez.

His computer was in the spare bedroom which he had set up as an office. "I'm not expecting any company," he'd told me long ago, "So I might as well utilize the space for my computer and all my files and stuff. It keeps the mess out of the living room and out of sight."

Though the rest of his apartment was fairly neat, at least for a man, he wallowed in disorder here. A beat-up old file cabinet and a folding table where his laptop sat and a worn-out swivel chair were the only pieces of furniture. Both the cabinet and the table had towering piles of files on them. On the floor stacks of bankers' boxes lined the perimeter of the room, and I wondered if he ever threw out a piece of paper in his entire life. Surprisingly he was able to put his hands on anything he wanted almost immediately. It was a magical feat as far as I was concerned.

He'd brought one of his dining chairs into the room so I could sit beside him as he trolled the Internet. It didn't take him long to find Roberto's Facebook page. Luckily his privacy controls were not activated.

"Okay, let's see what this young man is up to," he said.

We sat side by side as he scrolled down the page. A lot of it was silliness as far as I was concerned. University students seem more immature than ever to me, but I suppose every generation thinks that about those that follow them. A lot of the entries and pictures were about partying and drinking. I wondered if he'd heard the warnings about future employers checking out Facebook to get the lowdown on job seekers. If so, he was in trouble.

"Hey, look here," Ty pointed to the bottom of the page. I hadn't gotten there yet. "Roberto wants to buy a 1980s VW Bug. He asks if anyone has any leads on one."

"That sounds promising. Are you going to tell him you have one?"

"I'm going to give him my phone number and tell him to contact me because I know where he can find one."

Ty began typing his reply.

"I hope you aren't going to get a lot of crank calls by giving out your number like that," I said.

He shrugged. "That's a chance I have to take."

Shortly he closed up his laptop and sighed. "Now it's a matter of waiting for a reply."

"If you get one."

"How can he resist? The idea of finding a 1980s bug is too good to pass over."

"Let's hope."

AFTER LUNCH TY went to play bridge, and I went back to my apartment to do a washing and some other chores. I really needed to balance my checkbook, but I was so fidgety wondering if Roberto *or* Lawrence was going to call I knew I couldn't concentrate on figures. It drove me crazy that I spent half my life waiting around to hear from people.

Ty assured me he would take his phone while he played cards and let me know as soon as he heard something. He claimed he had someone on standby who could take his place should he hear from either Lawrence or Roberto with news that required us to act at once.

When we met in line for dinner he told me someone called him while he was playing bridge, but it wasn't Roberto. "It was some kid who saw my comment on the Facebook page and was trying to beat him to it. But I told him Roberto had first dibs. If he didn't want it, I'd call him back."

"So you had to lie to not one but two young kids."

He shrugged his shoulders. "The price of trying to get

information. What they don't know won't hurt them. Besides you're a fine one to talk. I think you've told many more lies these past few weeks than I have in a year."

"You got me there."

We had almost reached the buffet when his phone rang, or should I say played the Brown University Bears Fight Song. Ty stepped out of line and I followed him around the corner to the Arts and Crafts room.

From his end of the conversation I assumed it was Roberto since he said, "Can we meet this evening somewhere near the campus?"

And then, "Seven-thirty at the McDonald's at the corner of Walnut and Piedmont? That'll work. No, I won't be driving it there."

Finally he said, "Okay, see you then." He gave a fist pump when he hung up. Must have been the collegiate influence.

Later as we drove to the restaurant Ty suggested, "Let's be just Vi and Ty. No last names. It'll simplify matters."

"Do you think we should give our real names? They're not run-of-the-mill you know. What if he tells Billy he talked to us? I mean what's one more lie at this point?"

I don't think he recognized the sarcasm in my voice. "Hadn't thought of that. Okay, I'll be Tom. Who do you want to be?"

"I've always wanted to be Cordelia. Seems like a romantic name."

"Hope I can remember that."

The rest of the way I kept going over it in my mind— *Tom and Cordelia, Tom and Cordelia.* It would be really embarrassing to slip up.

Roberto had told Ty he'd be wearing a Cornwallis University T-shirt so we could identify him. He was sitting in a booth sipping a coke when we arrived. He stood up when we approached the table. Someone had taught him manners which is rare in this day and age. He was short in stature, slender, a handsome young Hispanic teen with a shy smile.

We slipped into the seat opposite him and introduced ourselves with our chosen names.

"Nice to meet you," he said pleasantly. "I'm Roberto of course." He had no accent. "So you know where I can find this Bug?"

"Before we get to that," Ty said, "We'd like to get to know you a little better. Where are you from Roberto?"

A brief look of concern flickered across his features. He probably wondered why we were asking personal questions. Had he been a victim of profiling? Since I'm of British descent, I couldn't imagine what it would be like to be instantly judged on your appearance, surely a demoralizing experience. Of course our motive for asking questions only to figure out if he would cooperate with us.

But then he relaxed and smiled, no doubt thinking two old codgers couldn't do him much harm. "I grew up in Hickory. My grandparents settled there from Mexico many years ago when my granddad got a job as a furniture maker. He learned to work with wood before he immigrated and was a skilled craftsman."

"I know it had to be traumatic when the furniture industry all moved to China," I said.

"Yeah, it was. But my granddad had already retired. So he didn't lose his job but it impacted his pension. They live with my folks now."

"So what are you studying?" Ty asked.

"I'm in pre-med."

"Fantastic," I said impressed. "Do you have your sights set on any particular med school?"

"I'd love to go to Duke. That's why I work so hard to keep my grades up."

I couldn't help thinking this was good and bad news. He seemed like a very upstanding young man who would want to do the right thing. On the other hand, he might not want to admit he knew Billy had started a fire and didn't report it. That could derail his ambitions for the future. From the look on Ty's face I knew he was having the same thoughts.

"It looks like you have a splendid future ahead of you, Roberto," Ty said. "You seem like a principled young man. I have a question for you."

Roberto frowned. "You mean this isn't about a VW Bug after all?"

"I'm afraid not. I needed to talk to you and it was the only way I could think of to get together."

The young man looked from Ty to me. There was definitely fear in his eyes now. "What could you possibly want from me?"

"We live in a nearby retirement center," Ty began. "About three weeks ago a fire destroyed the kitchen and damaged the dining room. The sad part is one of our residents is going to be charged with setting it."

"Incidentally," I said, "his arms were badly burned in the fire and he's been in the hospital ever since. I was able to talk with him and I'm convinced that he did not set it."

"So what has this got to do with me?" Roberto asked.

"Your roommate, Billy, was fired from the kitchen staff about a week prior to the fire. We've heard he was quite bitter about it and complained his loss of salary would hurt his ability to go to school." Ty was giving his best oratorical performance, adding as much drama as possible to what he was saying. "Cordelia and I feel there is a very good possibility that Billy set that fire out of anger.

We need to learn the truth before an innocent man is sent to jail for this act."

Roberto's eyes were wide with shock. "Oh my god, what a terrible thing." His surprise seemed genuine. "I don't know Billy very well even though we room together. We don't have a lot in common, and we spend very little time together. But I've had a feeling that he cheats on some of his papers and exams. He doesn't seem to be the most conscientious guy I've ever known."

"Has he ever said anything to you about Glendon Hills?" I asked. "Has he seemed vindictive about the loss of his job?"

"No. I knew he worked there though he didn't talk about it. Then suddenly he wasn't any longer, but he didn't say why."

It seemed evident Roberto knew nothing that could help us.

"Do you think there would be any way you could get him to talk to you about it? We have no evidence to help our friend so if you could get him to admit to you what he'd done, it would be our only hope," Ty said.

Roberto grimaced. "I don't know. It isn't like we hang out and share our inner thoughts. I'm afraid if I started to ask questions he would get suspicious."

It looked like we were getting nowhere, and I didn't feel we could push it any further. We'd just have to hope and pray Billy might make an incriminating statement in front of Roberto, but the odds seemed against it. "If you see or hear anything that sounds like it might help would you contact us?" I asked.

"I guess I could do that. But I'd be surprised if that happened."

I hunted in my purse for a small notebook I use to jot down grocery lists. I knew Ty didn't want to give him his card that had his real name on it. I tore out a sheet and wrote "Cordelia" and my phone number and handed it to him. "Just in case."

He took it reluctantly and stuck it in the pocket of his jeans. "Don't count on hearing from me. I'd like to help, but I doubt that I can."

Ty held his hands palms up in a pleading gesture. "If you could give us any pertinent information at all, maybe I could help you find your VW. I have a lot of contacts all over."

Roberto's face lit up. "No joke? That would be awesome."

"Can't make any promises, but I would certainly make the effort."

On the way home I asked Ty, "You weren't just feeding him another line were you? Could you really help him find a car?"

"Possibly. I've got friends around the country, and a few of them are car nuts. I think I could track something down."

"Do you feel like I do, Ty? Like we have fishing lines with big hooks dangling out there all over the place. Do you think we'll ever get a bite?"

"I guess it depends on how hungry the fish are."

TWENTY-SIX

WHEN I GOT back to my apartment there was a message from Lawrence on my phone. "I've called and called Roz. She either doesn't get my message or doesn't want to talk to me. I have a feeling it's the latter."

I called him back immediately. "I'm not surprised Roz won't talk to you," I told him. "She's probably still bitter about being fired. Did you try calling without leaving a message?"

"That's what I did at first. But knowing her she decided not to pick up when she saw my caller I.D. That sure makes it hard to get in touch with people who don't want to talk to you."

"Did you say in your message you had some back pay for her?"

"I did. She must have thought I was lying in order to get her to call me. God only knows what she thinks I would do to her. The girl is paranoid."

"So I guess either Ty or I need to call her since she won't recognize our names. Maybe she'll answer out of curiosity."

"But will she believe you when you tell her you have money for her?"

"If I can figure out some way of meeting her in person and have the money to show her. How can she resist when she sees a stack of bills?"

There was a moment of silence while Lawrence thought

about my suggestion. "I can't think of any other way to make this happen. If you could do this I'll be eternally grateful."

"I'm willing to give it a try. How can I get the money?"

"I don't keep that kind of cash on hand. Since it's Saturday, I can't get to the bank till Monday. Maybe you could set something up with her for Monday afternoon or evening."

"I'll do my best to make it happen."

"I can't believe you're willing to do all this for Deborah and me. You didn't even know us a couple of weeks ago. You and Ty are amazing people."

I didn't know how to respond to that so I said, "I'll let you know if I can arrange something with her. Bye for now," and hung up.

I sat on the sofa and petted Sweetie who had fallen asleep on my lap while I thought about how I could entice Rosalind to meet with us. When I couldn't come up with any ideas I decided to sleep on it.

SUNDAY IS BRUNCH day and I was looking forward to having waffles with strawberries again. We'd heard that the caterer was going to set up a waffle maker for the first time since so many residents favored them and ordered them every week. I'd heard there'd been grumbling last Sunday when all that was offered was fried chicken.

Ty as always chose good nutrition and had the baked white fish and Brussels sprouts. I wondered sometimes if he did that purely to make me feel bad. Well, I didn't. I relished every bite.

"I had a message from Lawrence last night," I told him after we were seated, "so I called him back."

"It sure took him long enough."

"That's because he couldn't reach Roz. She wouldn't

pick up when he called, and she never returned his messages. I'm sure when she saw his name she decided not to answer the phone."

"Gun-shy apparently."

"She must be really scared of something. Either that or pissed off."

Ty took a bite of Brussels sprouts. "Yum," He said, winking at me. He loved to taunt me about my food preferences. "You know, Vi, this whole thing is getting ridiculous. Why don't we go on a road trip and forget all this nonsense?"

I knew he wasn't serious. But I shared his frustration. "It's too hot to go anywhere. Anyway, I have one half-baked idea."

He frowned as he pulled little pieces off the fish with his fork. "You mean like this whitefish?"

"See, you should have gotten a waffle too. They can't do too much damage to them. Have a bite?" I offered him my fork with a piece of waffle but he waved it off.

"No, I'll eat a nutrition bar when I get back to my apartment. At least the sprouts are edible. So tell me about your idea."

"I thought if I called her she might answer since she won't recognize my name."

"Then what?"

"Then I have to entice her to meet with me. Lawrence is going to get me cash so I can show it to her and assure her she'll get the money if she helps us."

He finished his sprouts and small salad and pushed the plates away. "And how are you going to get this reclusive woman to meet with you? She seems to be hiding from everyone. She's going to wonder how you tracked her down."

"Well, here's my scenario. Don't know if it will work, so maybe you can come up with a better idea."

"Let's hear it."

"I'm going to tell her I met her brother when I was visiting a friend at the hospital and we got to chatting. The subject got around to the fact I'm having a hard time finding a good secretary who knows something about the advertising industry and he mentioned that his sister might be interested."

"Okay. That sounds like a good start. You said he told you she needed money so I assume she's not working. But how are you going to explain you want to meet her outside of an office?"

"I'm going to say I like to interview job applicants in an informal setting and I often take them to lunch."

He scratched his head as he considered that. "I guess that could work. So you want to do this alone?"

"I think so. Two of us might scare her off."

"So when are you going to call her?"

"Tonight. If she agrees I can give Lawrence a heads-up to get the money out of the bank and I'll stop by and pick it up on my way to meet her."

Ty gave a deep sigh. "Kind of hate having you go alone."

"I'll be in a restaurant surrounded by people. What could go wrong?"

He grimaced. "Don't even ask. Something can always go wrong."

"Wow. You're doom and gloom today."

"I know. Let's get out of here. I need a change of scenery. What shall we do?"

"I was thinking that Cliff might be wondering why we haven't been to see him since he got home."

"Just so we don't spill the beans."

"I'll be super careful."

Since Ty carries his cell phone with him, he called the Rineharts from the lobby. Greta answered and told him

Cliff was suffering from boredom and would love to have company. So he told her we'd be right over.

"What excuse can we give him for not visiting him sooner?" Ty asked. "It's been almost a week."

We were riding in Ty's car with the top down of course. I was glad we only had a few miles to go. Even with my pink sequined ball cap on, I knew I'd probably get sunburned. I hadn't bothered to go back to my apartment to apply lotion.

"Why don't we talk about Arthur Tisdale? Since Cliff's not involved with that case he'll think we're putting all our energy into helping him."

"That ought to keep him intrigued. Give him something to think about."

The Rineharts greeted us as though they hadn't seen us in weeks. I was touched by their enthusiasm. Greta already had a tray on the coffee table with a pitcher of iced tea and an assortment of fancy cookies.

Cliff looked really good. He'd lost a little weight, but since he'd put some on during the past two years, he was now back to where he'd been when I first moved here. I'm sure his doctor was pleased.

"You look terrific," I said. "How are you feeling?"

"Physically nearly back to normal. I'm just bored out of my mind."

"I practically have to tie him down to make sure he doesn't go back to work too soon," Greta said.

"I don't envy you," Ty said to her. "And just be forewarned—it's probably a preview of retirement."

"I don't intend to *ever* retire," Cliff proclaimed. "Greta would probably poison my orange juice if I did."

"You'd better believe it." She grinned and asked if we wanted coffee instead of tea. We told her tea was fine. "As long as there's no poison in it," I added.

"So what has kept you so busy you couldn't come and visit your poor old nephew-in-law?" I think he made up the term, but he always referred to himself that way.

"Are you trying to put me on a guilt trip?" I asked as I reached for a cookie.

"Damn right. You guys are retired. You must have all kinds of free time on your hands." He said it in a teasing way, but I knew deep down he really meant it.

"Cliff!" Greta frowned. "They came to see you and now you're scolding them. They'll never come back if you treat them that way."

He wasn't a bit cowed. "They're too busy driving around in that damn little car that's hardly big enough for midgets."

"Please do not cast aspersions on my automobile." Ty was getting into the swing of it. I hoped all this banter was helping Cliff get his frustrations off his chest. "I'll bet I can park in spaces where that boat of yours would never fit. And we won't even mention gas mileage!"

"Who cares? At least mine's comfortable." He looked at me as he said it expecting me to back him up. But I wasn't about to go there.

"All my life I wanted a convertible," I said. "Now I can ride in Ty's, and it's great fun." I hoped Ty didn't notice that I failed to say it was comfy.

"Enough already," Greta said. "They didn't come here to argue the merits of their car." She turned to me and said, "So what exciting things are going on at Glendon Hills?"

TWENTY-SEVEN

I WAS RELIEVED. Now I could talk about a non-controversial subject.

"You remember we told you about the fire at Glendon Hills," I said.

"Right," Greta said. "How on earth are they feeding you?"

"They've hired a caterer and have a buffet line in the community room where we used to do our exercises."

"How's the food?"

"Don't ask," Ty said. "We're not going to starve, but I can't say much for it beyond that."

"Didn't you say they thought the fire was deliberately set?" Cliff asked. Clearly the lawyer in him couldn't resist wanting to know who was accountable. I could almost imagine the wheels in his mind working overtime: Is this someone I could represent? What was his or her motive? What mitigating circumstances might there be? Is this a slam-dunk case?

"Yes," I said, "and apparently they're on the verge of arresting the resident who got burned that night. But I think they're on the wrong track."

Cliff looked at me with a sly smile. "I think I suggested you might want to get involved, but you said no way. Have you changed your mind?"

"I talked to Arthur, the man they suspect, and I believed him when he told me he didn't do it. His story was very compelling."

"If you weren't retired I'd hire you Vi. You can't resist getting involved can you?"

"Well I sure don't want to see an innocent person prosecuted."

Cliff was intrigued now and asked me many questions about why I had faith in Arthur and what were we going to do about it. I could tell his forced time off for recuperation was excruciating, and he missed the challenge of working with his clients. The vast majority of them were no doubt guilty, but the possibility that on rare occasions he might help exonerate an innocent client no doubt made up for all the deadbeats he represented. I realized how much it would have meant if he had been the one responsible for freeing Phyllis Duncan instead of nearly having her committed to a mental institution. It must have been galling that Ty and I, totally untrained in the law, led investigators to the real perpetrator. How would he feel if we did the same for Lawrence and Deborah? But I had to put that out of my mind for now.

"I learned that a busboy was fired shortly before the fire and thought it possible he could have been motivated to start the fire," I told Cliff. "One of our servers knew the first name of his roommate and Ty took it from there."

"First I had to con the university administration into giving me his last name" Ty said. "Then I looked him up online. A lot of these kids haven't bothered with the privacy settings on their Facebook page so that gave me the tip on how to entice him to meet with us."

"Ah, yes, privacy settings," Cliff nodded. "If people only knew how much the Internet helps both law enforcement and crooks they wouldn't be so free and easy with their personal information."

"Anyway," I added, "with the promise to help find an

eighties VW Bug, Roberto is going to do a little investigative work for us."

"So he came pretty cheap, eh?"

"Yes, thank goodness. It's not like we could afford to bribe somebody." As soon as I said it all I could think of was the five thousand dollars we had to bribe Rosalind to talk with us. I guess it would be nice if money was always available to loosen people's tongues, but unfortunately that rarely happens.

Speaking of bribes, it *almost* made me feel guilty we were working for the Rineharts with the promise of ten thousand dollars for our library. It undoubtedly would be the best retirement center library in the state with that kind of money. I want to be clear, though, I was convinced they were innocent or I wouldn't have considered accepting it. However, I was putting the cart before the horse; we had to solve the murder before our library would benefit.

When it came time to leave and we headed for the door, Greta took me by the arm and whispered in my ear, "This has done Cliff a world of good. He loves hearing what you guys are up to. Please come again soon."

I promised her I would. As we drove home, I told Ty what Greta had said.

"I wonder how he will feel if we tell him we've found the murderer in the Rinehart case? Do you think that would perk him up or put him in a blue funk?" Ty asked.

"We have to make it happen first," I reminded him. "We still seem to be a long way from doing it so I'm not going to worry about Cliff's reaction just yet."

THAT EVENING I fixed my traditional Sunday evening meal of toasted cheese sandwich and tomato soup which I ate in front of the TV while I watched the news and *60 Min-*

utes. All the while I gave myself a mental pep talk about calling Rosalind because so much hinged on the outcome of this phone call. If she didn't answer or answered and refused to talk to me, I didn't know where else we could go. I wondered if I was mistaken to consign so much importance to her role, but in the process of elimination she was the last one standing as far as I could see.

I finally worked up courage and dialed the number. It rang a number of times, and I was about to hang up when someone said, "Hello?" in a very tentative voice.

I was pretty sure I hadn't told her brother my name, but just in case I decided to call myself Cordelia Amherst. Since I like the name, I thought I might as well stick with it. Better than Vi-OH-la.

"I'd like to speak to Rosalind Voncannon," I said in my most businesslike tone.

There was a hesitation before she said softly, "Speaking."

I was afraid she might hang up at any moment so I got to the point fast.

"My name is Cordelia Amherst," I said, "and I met your brother Ted Bainbridge recently when I was visiting a friend in the hospital where he works. We got into quite a conversation, and I told him I'm with a start-up advertising company in High Point that's looking for experienced employees. He said you had worked as a secretary in an established agency in Guilford City and might be looking for a new position." I'd chosen High Point because of its proximity to Guilford City yet one could hide in plain sight there. The fact she'd cut off all communications with friends in Guilford City meant she had issues about staying in town.

"He gave you my number?"

"Yes, he did." I decided to lay it on thick. "He told me what a good worker you were and highly recommended you."

"Oh." There was surprise in her tone. "Well, I guess I'd be interested in interviewing for it."

All right! I was on a roll. "Since our office is just being decorated and not yet open, I'd like to take you to lunch."

"Okay."

"How about meeting me at Blue Water Grill on State Street at noon tomorrow?" I chose one of the best restaurants in High Point. I wanted her to think the fictional agency was a class act.

"I'll be there."

When I hung up I was elated. But I knew I had a daunting task ahead of me. If she was the guilty party, a bribe was not going to make her confess. But her reaction might tell me a whole lot. If she knew something about someone else, the five thousand dollars might be enough to get her talking.

TWENTY-EIGHT

When I met Ty in the café the next morning we were both brimming with news.

"You first," I told him. "I can tell you're dying to tell me something."

"I gotta give Roberto credit. That kid works fast," he said.

"You mean you got something on Billy?"

"It's looking pretty good. Hold on while I fix myself a cup of coffee."

I'd gotten there first and already had mine. Still I was impatient as I waited for him to fix his. When he sat back down he took his time opening a packet of sweetener and stirring it into his cup. I knew he was teasing me and I wanted to strangle him.

"Tell me already!" I finally lost my patience.

He grinned. "You'll never guess what gave him the opportunity to get the information."

"No guessing games. What?"

"They had a fire drill in the dorm, and Roberto was in the bathroom. When he came out, Billy had left and his laptop was on his desk. Roberto opened it and saw Billy had only closed the lid but hadn't turned it off in his haste to leave. It was a journal of some sort. He took the time to send a copy of it to his own laptop before he left the building."

"A fire drill. How ironic is that? So has he read it?"

"Roberto took his laptop to the library early this morning and read the whole thing. Billy has been keeping the journal since he was fired from GH. He ranted and raved about the unfairness of it all and then described how he managed to get into the building and set the fire. He hung out around the back entrance until a resident came with a swipe card and Billy boldly followed him in. The resident recognized him from the dining room and apparently hadn't realized he no longer worked here."

"And I guess whoever it was never put two and two together when the fire happened."

"For one thing, Billy hid out in a restroom for several hours so the fire didn't happen right away. The resident had no reason to suspect him."

"So was his intent to burn the building down?"

"Apparently not. He wanted it to be a nuisance and do enough damage to close it down briefly. He didn't expect anyone to get hurt. At least that's what he says in the journal. I doubt he even noticed the bottles of rum. And those are why the police are sure Arthur set it. They think he was using it as the accelerant."

"Is this enough evidence to arrest Billy?"

"I think the fact it's on Roberto's computer keeps it from being straightforward evidence. But I'm hoping it's enough to get a warrant so they can seize Billy's computer. That should nail it."

"So is Roberto going to the police with it?"

"Hold on, I need to heat this up a bit." Ty got up to get more coffee. It felt like he was trying to torment me by making me wait. Sometimes I think he's being passive-aggressive when it's probably nothing of the sort. It's just my impatient nature that makes me so judgmental.

When he sat back down he said, "I decided to meet Roberto this morning and take him and his computer over to Cliff's. We'll ask him for his advice on how to handle it.

He was so interested in hearing about the whole thing yesterday; he was like a kid in a candy store with no money to spend. I thought it might cheer him up."

"Good move, Ty. He'll be tickled to death to get involved. And he wouldn't need to go into his office or anything. It'll only be advice.'

"So that's my story. What about you?"

"I called Roz last night."

"Did she answer?"

"I was afraid she wasn't going to, but she picked up just before I was ready to hang up."

"What kind of impression did you get of her?"

I decided to play tit for tat with Ty. "You'll have to wait while I get a refill." I couldn't help chuckling to myself when I saw the frustration on his face. I took my time refilling my cup and stirring cream into it. It's a good thing I didn't have siblings when I was young. I probably would have taken every opportunity to torment them. I think sometimes Ty and I are in our second childhoods, enjoying the perks and pitfalls of having a substitute sister or brother for the ones we never had.

Back at the table I said, "She came across as insecure. Our conversation was brief but she's willing to meet me for lunch today for an 'interview.' I called Lawrence before I came downstairs and he's getting the money and bringing it here at eleven. Everything is going to hang on this meeting Ty. I'm so scared of blowing it."

"No you won't. You spent your entire career dealing with girls and their mothers. You know how to manipulate—no, that's not a good word—*control* circumstances for the best outcome. In the two years I've known you I've seen you handle sticky situations with great skill. If anyone can do it, you can."

I was flustered by his compliment. He probably didn't

mean all that anyway but was giving me a pep talk so I'd feel more secure.

"It looks like a big day," I said. "Do you think we can clear both cases in the next twenty-four hours?" I was thinking that if Cliff had a part in helping Arthur Tisdale, it might lessen the impact if we solved the Rinehart case. And if it could be done very soon, Cliff wouldn't feel he had somehow failed. After all he hadn't been able to work since his heart attack.

"That would be a miracle. I'll be happy if we can wrap up one and that would probably be the fire. I think the evidence is pretty solid there. As far as your lunch with Rosalind goes, we don't have much to work with except her disappearance. Let's hope the money will loosen her tongue and the five thousand bucks produces information relevant to the case and not some personal problem that is totally unrelated."

"Or she doesn't make up some cockamamie story that sends us on a wild goose chase. Oh, Ty, I'm getting more and more worried about this."

He stood up and came around and put his arm around my shoulder. "I'm not Superman and you're not Wonder Woman. All we can do is out best. If we fail, we fail."

I met Lawrence in the lobby at eleven and he handed me a thick envelope wrapped with a wide rubber band.

"Good luck Vi," he said. "I can't tell you how much it means to me that you're willing to do this."

"As long as you understand there's no guarantee this is going to work. She could even take us down the wrong path if she chooses to mislead us. I'd hate to think you spent all this money for nothing."

He shrugged. I had the feeling five thousand dollars was a pittance for him. "That's a chance I'm willing to take. I feel I'm running out of options." He reached into his back pocket, brought out his billfold, and took out a hundred dollar bill. "This is to pay for your lunches."

"It's not going to cost that much for lunch," I said.

"See that she gets all the wine she wants. Maybe it will loosen her tongue."

I laughed. "Or it might just put her to sleep."

He shook my hand and I felt the tremor of the Parkinson's. I suspected that the trauma he was going through had worsened his condition.

I went back to my apartment for my purse and keys and headed out to the Blue Water Grill.

I arrived about ten minutes before noon and told the hostess I was Cordelia Amherst and was expecting a guest. She brought a young woman to the table about five minutes later.

"Rosalind?" I asked.

She nodded as she sat down across from me.

I judged her to be in her mid-thirties, a wan-looking bottle blonde whose dark roots indicated either a loss of interest in her looks due to depression or lack of money to get her hair colored. Her eyes looked sunken with smudges of gray below them—lack of sleep? Her bright red lips formed a tight smile as if it took great effort to appear congenial. This woman obviously had problems.

"I'm glad you were able to meet with me today," I said. "Why don't we order some wine first before we get down to business?"

She looked relieved to have a few minutes reprieve. Though she was working hard to keep her nerves under control, it was painfully evident they were about to get the best of her. I couldn't blame her. She probably needed a job badly and though the economy had recovered some, the unemployment rate was still high. I felt sorry for her especially because I had no job to offer and was here under false pretenses. It was at times like this that I wondered why I had decided to play detective. There were some aspects of it that were unsavory like misrepresenting who I was. But, in the balance, if I could help the Rineharts it was worth it.

While we waited for our wine she sat looking down at the table and fiddled with the silverware. It was a good thing it wasn't a real interview because she would have flunked it already.

"So tell me a little about yourself, Rosalind," I said, trying to get her to relax before we got into the nitty-gritty.

She finally looked me in the eye. "What do you want to know?"

"Are you from around here? Where have you worked in the past? What are your ambitions?"

The waitress brought our wine before she could answer, and Rosalind drank it greedily as I sipped mine. She seemed glad for any interruption.

She finally said, "I grew up in Virginia and went to a community college there. Came to North Carolina about five years ago."

"May I ask what brought you here?"

A light blush suffused her face. "I followed a boyfriend here. Unfortunately that relationship didn't work out." She drank more wine. The glass was already half empty.

"I'm sorry. So where exactly did you work in advertising? Your brother didn't tell me."

She hesitated. I knew she was thinking I'd check out her story. "Uh, I worked at the Rinehart Agency in Guilford City for three years."

"And why did you leave?" I was waiting for her to make up some tale how it was someone else's fault or, knowing I'd find out the truth, try to put the best face on her firing.

"I was in the middle of a very uncomfortable situation

there. I felt I had to leave." She didn't look me in the eye as she said it.

I decided it was time to get down to business. "Look, Rosalind, I happen to know you were fired. I also know that you cut off all communications with your former co-workers. No one has been able to find you. Why is that?"

Her eyes opened wide in alarm. "How did…? She started to get up to leave.

I reached across the table. "Please, listen to me. This is very important. I need your help."

She was standing now and about to grab her purse. "No way."

I hastily reached into my pocketbook and pulled out the envelope with cash.

"See this?" I said. "There's a great deal of money in here if you will just talk to me."

She hesitated.

I pulled off the rubber band and opened the flap and showed her the stack of bills. Lawrence had filled it with low denomination bills to make it look impressive. Her eyes opened wide but she seemed glued to the spot.

"Come on, sit down. We can at least talk for a few minutes."

She finally slid back into her chair without taking her eyes off the envelope.

I put it on the table beside my plate, far enough away she couldn't grab it and run.

"So who are you? What do you want to know? This is no job interview, is it?"

TWENTY-NINE

"No it's not, Rosalind. I'm here because Lawrence and Deborah Rinehart have been charged in the death of Jeremy Scofield. I don't believe they did it, and I have a feeling you know something about it."

She seemed too shocked to respond. Because she didn't know or because I did?

"Well?"

She visibly pulled herself together. "I left the agency before that happened."

"But you know something about it."

She picked up her wine glass and drank all that was left. "Can I have more?"

"Absolutely." I signaled the waitress and Rosalind ordered a refill.

She sat there silently, her hands clasped on top of the table. She was attempting to stonewall me.

"Okay," I said. "If you want this money you're going to have to talk to me. What do you know?"

"Well, it was all over the paper. Everyone in town knows about it."

I shook my head. "That isn't going to fly. You know more than what was reported in the paper."

"How much money is in that envelope?"

"Five thousand dollars."

Her mouth dropped open. "What do I have to do to get it?"

The waitress brought her a new glass of wine, and she

immediately picked it up and drank most of it. If it had been me, I'd have been halfway tipsy by now, but Roz seemed to have a much greater tolerance for alcohol. I hoped that at least it might be oiling her tongue a bit.

"You have to tell me the truth about what you know. Is someone in the office responsible?"

She squirmed in her chair and looked uncomfortable. "I'm between a rock and a hard place."

"And where exactly is that?"

"My life has been threatened. Why do you think I disappeared?"

I stared into her eyes, daring her to lie to me. "You're saying you weren't involved but you know who was and they are threatening you?"

Tears began to slide down her face. She slowly nodded yes. I found a little packet of tissues from my purse and handed them to her. She pulled one out and wiped her eyes. Her mascara was now smeared under her eyes giving her the appearance of a waif.

I picked up the package with the money and waved it at her. "If you want this, Rosalind, you must talk to me."

"I want it—I *need* it badly, but I'm scared."

"Number one, no one will know you talked to me, at least not until the guilty party has been arrested. Two, you can't spend the rest of your life in hiding. Once the perpetrators are in jail, you won't have to hide any more. This is no way to live. We want you to have the money so you can start to rebuild your life, but you have to help us out."

She chewed on her fingernails for several minutes as she considered this. Finally she heaved a reluctant sigh and said, "If you're sure you can protect me."

"I'll do everything I can."

"Everybody hated him." She said in a righteous tone.

"You're talking about Jeremy?"

"Yes. He was a scumbag. No one could understand why Lawrence hired him."

"You're aware they'd known each other since college, aren't you? I think he had a sense of loyalty to him and wanted to help him out."

"Well, loyalty is fine but why foist him on the rest of us?"

The waitress approached us and asked if we were ready to order. We hadn't even looked at the menu yet so we asked her to give us a few minutes. I don't think either of us felt like eating at that point but after studying the menu we ordered anyway, a chopped prawn salad for Rosalind and a Mediterranean Ahi salad for me.

After the waitress left I had to prompt her again. "Okay, Rosalind, I'm waiting to hear the story."

"Well, Candy Knowlton called me one night. I'd lost my job about a week earlier but I was still in town. She said she and Missy Fenstermacher wanted me to meet them at the Arboretum and it was urgent. When I asked what it was about, she wouldn't tell me, but said they needed me right away. When I got there, the girls were almost hysterical. They took me down a path away from the parking lot to a bench near a tool shed. They led me behind the shed where Jeremy was lying, his head covered in blood. I couldn't believe it."

"You're sure he was dead then?"

"He sure looked it to me. I asked them what happened. Missy was a mess by this point and she couldn't even talk. We all knew Jeremy had been hitting on Missy until the day he was fired from the agency. Missy had been divorced for a number of years, and she was lonely and vulnerable. Even though she knew Jeremy was married, he told her the marriage was on the rocks and they were about to separate. He still called her after he was fired, and when he asked her to go out with him, she agreed because she wanted to have a little fun. She wasn't expecting to be raped, though. He practically poured drinks down her throat until she was too drunk to resist. She felt so humiliated and embarrassed she couldn't bring herself to report him. She felt that somehow she had brought it on herself."

What a sad tale. It sounded hauntingly similar to the story his wife's sister told me. How many times do women blame themselves when they are treated badly by men? Has it been bred into us that we are inferior creatures and that it's okay to abuse us?

"So they lured Jeremy to the park and killed him?" I asked.

"That wasn't the intention. Candy despised him as well, not only because he made lecherous remarks to her, but because of the accident caused by his drunk driving. The woman who was hurt was her cousin's best friend. Candy knew how much pain and suffering she'd gone through and how the injury had turned her life upside down. The more Candy and Missy talked about their hatred of Jeremy, the more they wanted to get some kind of revenge."

"What did they plan to do?" I was riveted by the story. Rosalind seemed to have forgotten her earlier hesitancy.

The waitress came with our salads, and Rosalind seemed startled when she set the plate in front of her. She'd become so involved in her story she'd forgotten where she was. I was hoping the interruption didn't cause her to rethink her willingness to cooperate.

"This looks good," she said. "I'm hungrier than I realized."

Once the waitress left I urged her on. "So what was their plan?" I asked again.

"Candy called Jeremy and said she missed him at the office and was sorry he was no longer there. It almost made her gag to say that. She told him she wondered if they could get together. She said he was practically panting over the idea. They arranged to meet at the Arboretum on a Friday night."

"Okay," I said remembering. "He told his wife he was going to Lawrence's house to get some back pay that night."

"He wasn't getting back pay, he was getting *payback*." Rosalind grinned for the first time. She was totally relaxed now thanks to two glasses of wine and the promise of the money.

We both took a minute to eat a few bites of our salads.

"Ummm, good," Rosalind said. "I never get to eat like this. What a treat."

"Don't get carried away. I want to hear the rest of the story."

"Both of the girls went to the Arboretum that night. Candy waited on the designated bench where she was to meet him. Missy hid behind the shed with a bucket full of dirty toilet water. Candice deliberately led him on until he began to tear at her clothes when Missy ran out and poured the stinky water over his head yelling, 'You scum. You belong in a sewer.'"

"That was a crazy thing to do," I said. "They were asking for trouble."

"I guess they hadn't thought it through very carefully. They figured two-to-one they'd be safe. But he was so enraged, he knocked Candy to the ground and started after Missy screaming he was going to kill her."

"Wasn't there anyone around who could have helped them?"

"No, it was after dark and they were the only ones in the park. Missy was sure he really *was* going to kill her. But Candy got to her feet, picked up a big rock from the edge of a flower bed and threw it at his head. He went down immediately and never stirred. She was afraid he could get up and hurt them, so she picked up the rock and hit him again as hard as she could to make sure he was out."

"But he was more than out, I presume. He was dead."

"That's what they finally realized. And that's when they called me."

"But why?"

"They tried to pick him up and carry him to the parking lot but he was too heavy. He was deadweight." At that she threw her head back and snorted at the unintended pun. I could tell the wine had gone to her head. "They needed me to help carry him. They wanted to get him into the car so they could take him to the river and throw him in. They knew his body would be discovered in the morning if they left him there because that Arboretum is so popular."

"And?"

"I told them no, I wouldn't get involved in anything like that."

"So what did they do?"

"I honestly don't know because I left. But they did threaten me. They said if I told anyone what happened, they'd come after me."

"Did you really think they'd harm you?"

"I wasn't going to take a chance. I gave up my apartment, got rid of the old cell phone, cut all ties. I wanted to keep as low a profile as possible."

"You might not know this, but they found Jeremy's hair on a tarp in the Rinehart's garage and his blood in the trunk of their car."

Rosalind looked shocked. "How on earth…?"

"I have no idea. If it happened the way you just described it, Missy and Candy must have gotten help in moving the body and planting the evidence. Do you think either of them have a vendetta against the Rineharts?"

She shook her head no. "Not that I was ever aware of. My god."

We both turned to our salads as we thought about this. Mine was so good I decided to urge Ty to come here with me some day as a treat.

"Another thing," I said, "if they planned to throw him in the river, I wonder why he ended up in Pinewood Park behind Glendon Hills where I live?"

"Oh, do you live there? I had an aunt in the nursing home there at one time. Nice place. But that's a retirement center. Why are you involved with the Rineharts?"

"It just happened that Leah Rinehart and I were searching in the woods for my cat when we found Jeremy's body. The park backs up to my building. And Leah asked me to get involved when it looked like the Rineharts would be charged."

"So you're friends with the ex-Mrs. Rinehart?"

I wasn't going to go through a prolonged explanation so I just said yes.

"This gets curiouser and curiouser. I'm surprised she wants to help Lawrence after he left her for Deborah."

"They have an amicable relationship. She certainly doesn't want to see them found guilty of this murder."

"Well, I don't either. But I want my name kept out of this. I've told you everything I know."

"Will you tell me where you live?"

"No. I worked hard to cover my tracks and I want it to stay that way for now. You have my phone number so you can reach me. But please don't give it out."

"You won't change phones will you?"

"No, I promise as long as you give me the money."

There was nothing I could do but take her word that

she'd do as she said. If what she told me was true, I knew who the perps were but not how they disposed of the body nor put the evidence at the Rinehart's home. If only they had reported it at the time, they probably could have pleaded self defense. But now they'd gotten themselves in really deep.

THIRTY

WHEN I GOT home a wave of exhaustion swept over me. It wasn't that I'd done anything physical to warrant being tired, but I felt as though I'd been walking an emotional tightrope with Rosalind. At least she'd finally opened up and told me her story. Since she had no idea what I was going to ask her, I doubt she made it up unless she was a master at dissembling, and I don't believe she had the smarts for that. It was all I had to go on, and I hoped I had enough to eventually answer all the questions.

I called Ty and we arranged to meet in the exercise room, "unless someone else is there," he said. "In that case the café is the next best place for privacy."

"I know Lawrence and Deborah will be chomping at the bit to hear from me, but I want to tell you what happened with Roz first. And I want to hear what happened with you and Roberto."

Luckily we had the room to ourselves.

"I feel beat," I said. "Dealing with Roz was like a workout in itself. Let's do the SciFit machines instead of the treadmills." These are like stationary bikes where you sit and pump the pedals while working your arms up and down with the handles.

"You first," I said once we were seated and had our machines in motion. I not only wanted to know what they'd decided to do with Billy's journal, but if it seemed to help Cliff's agitation to get back to work.

"Well, first of all, it was a big day for Roberto. He got

to ride in my car, which he said was almost as cool as a VW Bug, then he got inside one of the nicest homes in Guilford City. He was pretty impressed. And he had never met a criminal lawyer so that was a big plus too."

"What did Cliff think about the journal? Did he believe there's enough evidence to prosecute Billy?"

"He thought there was a good chance it would at least allow them to issue a warrant to seize his computer. So he called someone he knew at the police department and explained the situation to him."

"It helps to have an inside track," I said. "That's what you and I lack."

Ty laughed. "I guess Cliff is the closest we have to one, and we aren't always working with him but against him at times."

"So what did his contact at the police department say?"

"He said for us to bring Roberto's computer down to the station so they could look at it."

I was getting tired of the Scifit so I suggested we go to the weight machines. I took the one that strengthens the upper legs and Ty settled into the one that works out the arms.

"So you and Roberto went down to the police station. What happened there?"

"They told him they needed to keep his laptop for the day and he could go back tomorrow and pick it up."

"That's tough for a college student to give up his computer at all," I said. "How is he going to manage?"

"He said he could use one in the university library. He'd downloaded all his files before he left and had them on a flash drive, so he isn't terribly inconvenienced."

I chuckled to myself.

"What are you laughing about?" Ty demanded.

"Oh, I was hoping there wasn't any embarrassing material on his laptop he wouldn't want the cops to see."

"I imagine he thought of that beforehand and deleted anything that could be awkward. At least I hope he did."

"Okay, I've had enough of this one," I said climbing off my machine and we traded.

"So how did Cliff react? Do you think it did him any good?" I asked.

"I wish you could have seen him, Vi. He was like a kid at his own birthday party. He reveled in being included in this. Poor guy. If he doesn't go back to work soon I think Greta might shoot him or vice versa. They are really getting on each others' nerves."

"I think he really meant it when he said he was never going to retire."

"I hope he meant it for Greta's sake."

"You think you might know by tomorrow whether the police are going to act on what they find on his Roberto's computer?"

"I hope so. All we can do is wait and see. Okay, Vi, it's your turn. How did you and Rosalind get along?"

"She was about to leave when I revealed why I was there, but once I waved the money in front of her she decided to cooperate."

"Money usually talks, doesn't it? Or finding someone a used VW Bug."

"I'm sure she wouldn't have confided in me otherwise, but she needs the money badly."

"Do you think she's the one who killed Jeremy?"

"If I'm to believe her, and I really thought she was telling the truth, it was Missy and Candice. And it was self defense."

Ty stopped pumping his legs and looked at me in shock.

"The two of them? Self defense? How the heck did that happen?"

I repeated the story that Rosalind had told me. "She's scared they'll do something to hurt her if she tells the authorities. That's why she disappeared."

"But she has no idea how they got his body over to the park or the blood and hair evidence to the Rinehart's house."

"That's what she says. And I believe her, Ty. She didn't have a chance to think up this story in advance. And I don't think she's clever enough to have thought it up on the spot. She really seemed frightened too."

"So what we've got to figure out is who helped them move the body. And whoever that is probably planted the evidence."

"I think you've got it in a nutshell. But it almost feels like we're back to square one."

"No, not at all. We're at least halfway there which is a lot farther than we were a day ago."

I stopped pumping my arms. "I think it's time we called Lawrence and Deborah."

"Maybe it's time to take all this to the police, Vi. At least we know how Jeremy was killed."

"We started this, Ty. And I want to get to the bottom of it. I think we need to find out who moved the body and especially why they planted the evidence at the Rinehart's before we turn it over to the authorities. If we can find that out maybe they won't come down so hard on Missy and Candice. We've been working on this for so long I want to take it to its conclusion. It's a matter of pride now."

"I guess I have to agree. I have my handy dandy little phone right here," Ty said as he pulled it from the case on his belt. "Let me give the Rineharts a call."

THIRTY-ONE

According to Ty Lawrence told him, "We're so anxious to hear what transpired. Please come as soon as you can."

"'Transpired?' huh? No wonder he's in advertising with a vocabulary like that."

We didn't even bother to change our clothes but drove directly to the Rinehart home in our exercise outfits.

They both were at the door to greet us when we arrived. First Deborah then Lawrence gave me a hug and shook hands with Ty.

Back in the living room both of the Rineharts perched on the edge of the couch in anticipation.

"So did Rosalind show up?" Lawrence asked.

"Did you talk with her?" Deborah asked almost simultaneously.

"Yes and yes," I said.

"Where is she living now?" Lawrence asked.

"She wouldn't tell me. I still only have her phone number. She was ready to leave when I revealed who I was."

"Who did she think you were?" Deborah asked. "Did you make something up?"

"I had to reel her in some way. I said I'd met her brother and told him I was looking to hire someone experienced in advertising and he gave me her phone number."

"Pretty sweet," Lawrence said.

"But as soon as I started with the personal questions she almost left until I waved the money under her nose."

"I figured that was the key," Lawrence said.

"Money well spent," added Deborah.

"Well, then let me tell you her story." Again I related what Roz had told me about Missy and Candice. By the time I finished my tale the Rineharts were almost speechless.

"I can't believe they would do anything so stupid," Deborah raved. "What were they thinking?"

"People often throw common sense out the window when they're obsessed with having revenge," Ty said. "They're so bent on payback they don't even think what the consequences could be."

Lawrence sat shaking his head as though he were unable to process it. "And to think they come to work every day acting as though nothing had happened. That's what galls me. Do you believe Rosalind's story?"

"I really do," I said. "I don't think she could make up something like that on the spot."

"Oh, my god. To think I valued them as good employees and they stabbed me in the back."

"I'm not so sure they're the ones who planted the evidence," I said. "They had to find someone else to help them move the body when Rosalind refused to do so. I think that person must have done it, and they were in so deep by then they couldn't point the finger."

"So we have to figure who that person might be," Deborah said, brightening up a little as the possibility of solving this seemed a little closer.

"You know these two women better than we do," Ty said. "When Vi interviewed them, she only asked about Rosalind so she didn't learn a whole lot about either of them. What ideas do you have?"

Both Lawrence and Deborah retreated into their minds as they thought this over. Finally Lawrence said, "I think they would have needed a man to help them move the body. Especially since Jeremy was found so far out in the woods in that park. The two women couldn't have carried or dragged him that far by themselves."

"Are there any men at your agency who had a grudge against Jeremy? Someone the women might have thought could help them?" I asked.

"No. The guys didn't like him but they pretty much ignored him. As long as he stayed away from their wives or girlfriends, they didn't want to get involved."

"So you don't think he hit on any of their significant others?"

"I think he had his hands full putting the moves on the women in the office. I don't know why I was so blind. We were covered up with work at the time, and I hired Jeremy partly because I desperately needed the help and he had experience, and partly because I felt sorry for him. Unfortunately the women never complained to me how he was treating them, I guess because of our long-standing friendship. If I'd only known I would have canned his ass long before I did." He flushed a little. "Excuse my language, Vi."

"I've heard much worse language than that," I laughed. "Doesn't bother me. So what other man might they turn to?"

"Missy has been divorced for years, and I don't know that she's dating anyone now. Probably not if she went out with Jeremy."

"What about a father or brothers?"

"Her father would be far too old and she only has a couple of sisters who live out of state."

"So we go to Candice," Ty said.

"Candice!" Deborah said. "Candice has a husband."

"But why wouldn't they call him first instead of Rosalind?" Ty asked. "That would have been the logical thing to do."

"Because they're separating and she's going to file for a divorce," Lawrence said.

"What?!" asked Deborah. "I didn't know that. Why didn't you tell me, Lawrence?"

"Because she swore me to secrecy. She didn't want the people in the office gossiping about her."

Deborah scowled. "But, I'm your wife. You could have told me."

Lawrence leaned over and kissed her on the cheek. "When someone swears me to secrecy I figure that means I can't tell anyone, even you, darling. I'm sorry."

Deborah didn't say anything but still looked annoyed.

I decided I'd better get the conversation going away from the subject. "If they were desperate for help they might have called on him, don't you think?"

"That's a possibility," Lawrence acknowledged.

"Which brings up a question," Ty said. "If Candice's husband...what's his name?"

"Tom," answered Deborah.

"If Tom helped them dump the body in the park, wouldn't he probably be the one to put the evidence at your house?" Ty asked. "Or do you think one of the women did it?"

"I don't think Missy or Candice would do something like that," Lawrence said. "They've both worked for me for many years, and we've always had a good relationship. What do you think, Deborah?"

"I agree. I'd be shocked if it turned out to be them."

"What do you know about Tom?" I asked. "Have you been around him much? Do you know why they're divorcing?"

"The only time I've ever seen him is at our Christmas

parties. I know he works for a builder doing finish carpentry work," Lawrence said. "Honey, has Candice ever told you anything about him?"

"All I heard was he didn't have much work during the economic downturn. I think he was a house husband for a while taking care of those three kids. I can imagine that wasn't a lot of fun. But she told me about six months ago that the builder was starting to put up houses again, and he was back on the job."

"We have to think about this," I said. "If Tom did help the women move the body, why would he put evidence in your garage?"

"And how could he do it?" Ty added.

"For one thing," Lawrence said, "he'd want to direct the attention of the police away from the women and himself. And, as I think I told you when this all began, the back window of the garage is open to allow a little circulation of air. It gets to be a hot box in the summer."

"So he could have come in that way and seen the tarp and put the hairs on it," Ty went on. "How about getting in your trunk?"

"I think I emptied groceries out of it a day or two earlier," Greta said, "and I didn't lock it. Since it was in the garage with the door down I don't usually worry about it."

"So it really wasn't all that hard to plant the evidence," I said.

"How did he get the blood?" Ty asked.

"Jeremy's head was covered with it," I said. "If he'd just been killed the blood wouldn't have coagulated yet, and he could have easily gotten a small amount along with the hairs."

"This all sounds plausible," Lawrence said. "But surely those two women wouldn't have wanted to make me the perpetrator. I thought I'd always been good to them."

"Probably Tom said he'd put the evidence somewhere to mislead the investigators. I doubt he told them he was going to plant it at your house. And when they found out what he'd done, there wasn't much they could do without implicating themselves."

"Why on earth didn't they go to the police when it happened and tell them it was self defense?" asked Deborah echoing what I'd said earlier.

"I imagine they were too scared and afraid no one would believe them," Ty said. "After that it was too late."

"Well, this all sounds quite plausible, but we haven't an ounce of evidence to prove our theory," I said. "And of course we could be dead wrong about the whole thing."

Lawrence held his head in his hands in a state of despair. "Oh god, now what do we do? It all seems so hopeless. They're going to put us in jail and throw away the key."

THIRTY-TWO

"HOLD ON," I SAID. "Don't give up yet. We've gotten this far, I feel sure we can see this through to the end."

He looked up at me, his expression grim. "How?"

"Can you find out where Tom is living now? Better not ask Candice or she might get suspicious. Go through the builder he works for and make up some reason you want to get in touch."

"What then?" asked Deborah. She was looking as hopeless as her husband.

"I'm not sure yet. But Ty and I will come up with something."

I glanced at him and he shrugged his shoulders. I was glad the Rineharts were too busy with their worries to notice. I surreptitiously nodded toward the front door, and we stood up in tandem.

"You're up to date now," I said. "We'll be waiting to hear from you on Tom's whereabouts. Don't be discouraged. We've come a long way so far and we'll get to the bottom of it."

Deborah and Lawrence rose to their feet as if a crushing burden was riding on their shoulders. The thought that their valued employees had put them in such a dire position had to be devastating.

They walked us to the door.

"Thanks you two," Lawrence said. "You've done wonders so far. We can't thank you enough."

"Think positive," I said and then cringed inwardly at the cliché. But I couldn't think of anything else to say.

We were both quiet on the way home. I was wondering what we would do next. I felt our only hope was to contact Tom Knowlton. Then we'd have to figure how to get the truth out of him. That seemed almost beyond our ability.

There was a concert that evening in our multi-purpose room, a pianist and tenor performing lieder from Schubert and Schumann. It was just what we needed to get our minds off the Rineharts. I'm forever grateful to Glendon Hills for the entertainment they provide for us which can range from classical music to the big band sound. There's usually something to suit everyone.

WE WERE BOTH worn-out from our Monday meetings with Rosalind, Roberto and Cliff, and the Rineharts and decided we'd sleep in Tuesday morning and simply take it easy.

"I'll see if the Bridge Dudes are playing," Ty said when we parted the night before. "Bridge is the best thing I can think of to chill out. You should try it, Vi."

"Thanks but no thanks. I'd rather read or play solitaire. Don't worry about me."

I played bridge in college many years ago but found I didn't have the patience for it. Too much depended on the lay of the cards. If you had a lousy hand there was not much you could do. Of course there were days I felt we were dealt more than a lousy hand with the death of Jeremy Scofield, but I still wouldn't give up on that.

We met for supper and while standing in line for the buffet heard that the kitchen should be back in business in another week or so. To celebrate even Ty had dessert which sort of made up for the meatloaf that tasted as if it was mostly bread crumbs and overcooked green beans. As we were eating, Cora Lee came over to us. She's like a homing device, always able to find us no matter how far away from her we're sitting. She must have some kind of internal radar system.

"I hear they're about to arrest Arthur Tisdale," she said hanging over the back of my chair making me very uncomfortable. I couldn't look her in the eye without practically breaking my neck.

"Where'd you hear that?" Ty asked. He was always trying to figure out if she actually heard a rumor or simply made it up.

"Oh, just around. Everyone's talking about it."

When she left I asked Ty, "Did she have to seem so gleeful about it?"

"Cora Lee? Of, course. She thrives on stuff like that."

"Do you really think it's true? Have you heard from Cliff?"

"No, I haven't. I'll call him this evening."

I prayed our efforts were not going to be in vain. It seemed to me that the evidence was there if they'd just look at it.

About an hour after we returned to our apartments Ty called and said he'd talked to Cliff.

"The police said the case is still open and they're looking at additional evidence. They wouldn't be specific about it but he thinks they've probably subpoenaed Billy's laptop and are checking it out. It doesn't sound like they're about to pick up Arthur. God knows where these rumors start."

"In the minds of mischief makers," I said.

A couple of hours later close to my bedtime I got a phone call from Lawrence.

"I managed to track down Tom Knowlton. I have his address and phone number. I hope it will do you some good. But for heaven's sake, Vi, don't put yourself in jeopardy. I'd never forgive myself if anything happened to you or Ty.

"Believe me," I said, "neither of us is going to take any chances. We're too chicken for that."

I took down the information but decided it was too late to do anything about it. I'd wait till morning to talk to Ty so we could come up with a plan. This might be the trickiest part of the investigation yet.

The next morning in the café we drank coffee and threw out various scenarios that we might use to trap Tom. Some of them seemed impossible, others improbable, and then there were the downright dangerous ideas which we immediately discarded.

"I don't see how in the heck we'll ever get him to admit he planted the evidence," I said.

"We don't even know for sure that he did. It just seems like the most likely thing that happened. But they could have found someone else to help them."

"If it's not Tom, I think the game is over, Ty. There's no way to find out who else could have been involved."

"We can't get bogged down in negative thoughts. Let's just assume it's Tom and figure out how to approach him. There's got to be some kind of a foolproof and safe way to do that."

By my third cup of coffee I had an idea.

"Okay," I said, "let me run this by you. I think it has the least amount of risk and the most potential to catch him."

"What is this great idea?"

"Either Lawrence or Deborah said Tom was a finish carpenter. That means he builds things like cabinets and bookcases and such. Why don't we pose as a couple living here and ask him to give us an estimate on a bookcase for one of our apartments. I'm thinking let's use yours since it looks better than mine."

"Is that a compliment?"

"I guess. You have new furniture and I have second-hand stuff. Besides you have more of an eye for decoration than I do."

Ty rubbed his eyes and sighed. "Get to the point, will you Vi?"

"Sorry," I said sipping from my cup. "We'll pose as a couple because it's safer that way. And when he comes, I'll offer him a glass of iced tea and some cookies."

"This is not a social event."

I do believe he was beginning to get short-tempered. Of course I was egging him on a bit. "I know that Ty. The point is we'll have his fingerprints on the glass, and maybe I can serve something on a small plate that he'd have to hold as well."

Ty was beginning to perk up now. "Fingerprints! I hadn't thought of that."

"Surely Tom would have left fingerprints on Lawrence's car, especially the trunk, when he was planting the blood. On the tarp as well. I don't think he would have thought of wearing gloves because his prints probably aren't in the system."

"And the cops must have taken prints from the car. Brilliant Vi. I wish I'd thought of that."

'What do you say? Shall we go for it?"

"Absolutely. We have nothing to lose."

THIRTY-THREE

WE DECIDED TY should call Tom as soon as possible and ask him to come out to Glendon Hills.

"I'm sure he's working today," Ty said. "I'll call him this evening. Let's hope he's willing to take on extra jobs or he could just turn us down."

"Tell him he might get additional work here when other residents see what he can do for us. Make it sound really lucrative."

He grinned. "It always seems to boil down to money, doesn't it?"

"What can I say? Lawrence bribed us with a possible ten thousand dollars for our library."

"I'd kind of forgotten about that. I just do it because it's challenging. I was worried about being bored when I retired but, thanks to you Vi, that hasn't happened yet."

"So how are we going to challenge ourselves today? Everything is sort of on hold until you reach Tom, so what shall we do? I spent yesterday reading. I want to do something fun today."

"There's a place I've wanted to visit for a long time, and today would be a perfect day for it," Ty said.

"What's that?"

"Have you ever heard of Old Salem over in Winston-Salem? It's been restored to the way it was when the Moravians settled it in the early eighteen hundreds. There's even a tavern where we can have lunch. Everyone's in costume and some are working in the old crafts like making shoes and baking in an open wood-fired oven. I'm sure you've heard of Moravian cookies. Those wafer-thin molasses cookies?"

"Oh, yes, my favorite. And that's where the Moravian star comes from. I've always wanted one to hang on my balcony at Christmas."

The trip was just what we needed to restore our equilibrium after all we'd been through the past few weeks.

"That was a nice break from the caterer's food," I said on the way home in the late afternoon. We'd had a lovely lunch in the tavern. "I hope they were right when they said our kitchen would be up and running soon."

"I always thought our meals were good at GH," Ty said, "but I've learned to truly appreciate them after having to eat downstairs. That got old very fast."

"I'll bet there will be a lot fewer complaints once we get back in our dining room."

"I wonder what Arthur Tisdale will do if we get him off the hook. I don't think he'll have the nerve to complain after what happened to him."

I laughed. "I don't think so either. I would hope he learned his lesson. What you say can come back and bite you."

When we arrived back at Glendon Hills Ty asked if I would come to his apartment while he called Tom Knowlton. "I want you to be there to hear the conversation. Since we're posing as husband and wife he might have a question for you."

When we got to his place we discussed what he should say.

"Do you think I should tell him we need a bookcase for over there?" Ty pointed to a spot beside the large window on the back wall that overlooked the woods. He has virtually the same view as I do only from the other end of the building.

"Why not one on either side of the window? Let's make it worth his while. We could even say we want a bench under the window connecting the two so you'd have almost a full wall of built-ins."

Ty looked thoughtful as he stared at the space. "You know, Vi, that is a great idea. Maybe I'll really get someone to do that later."

"If you're serious about it, it will seem even more realistic when we talk to him"

He dialed the number he had for Tom, and we both crossed our fingers praying he'd answer. He finally did just as I began to fear this wasn't going to work at all.

Ty explained who he was and said he'd heard great things about his carpentry skills. Tom must have asked who he heard it from because Ty said, "a friend of a friend. One of those word-of-mouth things. Can't really think of his name now."

He went on to describe the built-in bookcases and window seat we wanted and stressed that he was looking for a "quality job" which translated to "spare no expense."

He listened some more before saying, "There are a lot of people here at Glendon Hills who are anxious to have some carpentry work done but don't know who to call. If you can do the job for us, I'd be happy to give your name out to our other residents. I'm sure you could get a lot of jobs out of it."

Finally the conversation closed with the promise that Tom would be here the next night to give us an estimate.

"All right!" Ty pumped his fist into the air when he hung up. "He's coming at seven-thirty tomorrow night. Why don't you come around seven to get the tea and cookies ready. Shall we go to the grocery tomorrow to pick up what we need?"

"You go play bridge. It doesn't take the two of us to do that. I need some other things and I'll get the food."

"You're a very understanding 'wife,'" he said grinning.

THE NEXT DAY I bought some delicious-looking chocolate macadamia-nut cookies in the bakery section that I hoped Tom couldn't resist as well as some ready-made sweetened tea, fancy paper napkins, and a box of large baggies to put the glass in after he touched it. I was hoping that fingerprints could be lifted from the napkins, too, though I wasn't sure. But I was going to use every tool I had to get the evidence we needed.

Dinner was our low point when we saw that the meal consisted of hotdogs, chips and coleslaw.

"Quite a comedown from yesterday isn't it?" asked Ty.

"Well, yeah. But we'll just pretend we're on a picnic. In fact, why don't we take our meals outside and sit on Lester's bench?"

"It's hot as Hades."

"I don't care. There's got to be a little breeze stirring."

We'd only been out there a few minutes when Ginger Willard came toward us holding a bouquet of flowers tied with a ribbon.

"I see you're sitting on my darling Lester's bench," she said as she approached.

"Yes," I said. "It's a nice addition to the area, a lovely place to sit and enjoy the birds and the view of the woods."

"Well, I take a new bunch of flowers to put on his grave every week or two. Just so he knows I'm thinking of him." And she headed toward the woods where she'd buried her pet parrot.

Ty and I looked at each other and tried to keep a straight

face. Apparently she'd been laying flowers on the bird's grave for the past four months. All I could think was it takes all kinds. I hoped someone would miss me as much as she misses that foul-talking parrot.

When we were through eating Ty suggested I pick up the tea and cookies from my apartment and come on to his. "Tom could turn up early. Anyway, we can play double solitaire till he comes."

I was at his apartment twenty minutes later carrying my groceries and a double deck of cards. I knew the Bridge Dudes furnished their own cards and he probably had none of his own.

Before we started to play he helped me set out glasses and plates. I wanted to serve the cookies on small individual plates that Tom would have to hold while he drank his tea. The more fingerprints the better.

We'd only been playing solitaire a few minutes when the doorbell rang. Ty went to answer it, and came back to the living room with a great hulk of a man. He wore his dark hair shoulder-length and had the day-or-two growth of beard that seems so popular with macho men. His eyes were a startling blue and gave me the eerie feeling he could look right into my mind. At his size and bulk he could have easily moved Jeremy from the Arboretum and taken him far into the woods of the park probably without assistance. I wished I had one of those life alert necklaces people wear in case he somehow figured out what we were up to. There are always security people in our building, but you have to pull a cord in the bathroom or bedroom to alert them, and I wasn't sure I could get there in time should worse come to worse. Then I chided myself for being so paranoid. This would probably go as smooth as glass.

THIRTY-FOUR

"THIS IS MY WIFE, Vi," Ty introduced me before he indicated a chair for Tom while we sat down next to each other on the couch. We wanted to appear like old married folks who are still sweet on each other.

"We're so glad you agreed to come," Ty told him. He gestured toward the window. "We want built-in book shelves all around the window and up to the ceiling."

"But, dear," I said turning to Ty, "remember we want cabinets with doors on the bottom." I laughed girlishly as I explained to Tom, "So we can hide our messy stuff."

"And don't forget the window seat underneath the window." Ty patted my hand as if perhaps *I* was the one who was a little forgetful.

"Yes, of course, darling. And we want it to have storage space in it as well. You know, a seat on a hinge that can be opened up. Don't you think that will just *make* this room, Tom?" I threw out my arms gesturing toward the window as if I were a fairy godmother and could bring it all to life with my magic dust.

Tom scowled a little and rubbed his chin thoughtfully. "That's quite a big job."

"We know you have a day job," Ty said, "and it might take a while to complete it, but we're so desperate for a place to put our books we're willing to wait as long as it takes. We need to get those boxes of books out of storage and on the shelves where we can get to them."

"Well…" Tom said, "the construction business isn't up

to full speed yet, so I might have some time during the day now and then and weekends I'm free. I think I could probably do it for you if you're not in a huge rush."

"Oh, not at all," Ty said. "And as I told you on the phone there are lots of people here looking for a carpenter who does good work. I know a couple of painters who've done very well here by word of mouth."

"Let me do some measuring," Tom said. "I can probably get back to you with an estimate in the next couple of days."

"That would be great," Ty exclaimed with great enthusiasm.

I thrust my hand out toward Tom like a cop stopping traffic "Wait now. Before you start, I made some delicious cookies and I have some iced tea. It's so hot out today I know you would like some refreshments."

"Well, ma'am, don't go to all that trouble. I'll just do my measuring."

I scrunched my face up like I was about to cry. "But, *Tom*, I made these especially for you. And I've found that all Southerners love their sweet iced tea. I'm from New England, so I'm learning what you all like to eat down here."

I knew I sounded like some kind of idiot, but I wasn't going to let him get away with refusing the food. I was already on my feet headed for the kitchen. "I've got it all ready to go. It will give us a chance to chat for a minute."

Out of the corner of my eye I could see Ty shrug as if he'd learned to put up with my odd little ways. "She loves to cook," he explained, "and she rarely gets a chance to bake for company. She spent the afternoon making these." We were putting such a guilt trip on Tom that he could hardly turn me down.

I came back with a plate in each hand holding two cookies apiece and handed them to the men. Then I poured the tea in the kitchen and brought out the glasses. I'd already put coasters on the end and coffee tables so it wouldn't ruin Ty's furniture. By the time I came back with my own tea and cookies, Tom was biting into one of his. I was hoping it was tasty because I bought the most expensive ones they had.

"This is very good, Mrs. Lan...?" Tom stumbled over the name.

"Landowski," Ty said. "Good old Polish name."

"Thank you," I said, "I'm so glad you like them." Truth be told I hadn't baked a cookie in probably twenty years. After all I always had a stash of Girl Scout cookies in my pantry.

Tom finished off both cookies and drank the whole glass of tea before getting up to measure the area where he was going to build our mythical bookcase. It took him a half hour to get all the measurements. I was beginning to breathe easier because it all seemed to be going smoothly.

Then as I watched him work and noticed how the muscles rippled in his arms I began to worry. If the fingerprints were instrumental in having him arrested, would he be able to figure out where those prints had come from? He did, after all, know where we lived.

Finally he said, "I've got all the measurements I need. I'll call you in a day or two and let you know what it will cost."

"Wonderful!" Ty enthused.

"Would you like some more cookies to take with you?" I asked.

"No thanks. But they were delicious. Your husband must be a happy man with a cook like you."

I smiled graciously but didn't say anything. I thought

we were both going to burst our seams trying not to laugh until he had left.

After the door closed Ty put his arm around my shoulder. "Such a great little cook. I feel guilty you had to slave over the stove on such a hot day."

"Okay, smarty pants. Let's get his glass and plate into some baggies. I'll stick the napkin in too just in case."

"I hope to god this works. If it doesn't, what am I going to do when he calls me up with the estimate and I have to tell him I've changed my mind? After all that buildup giving him the impression I want it at any price, that's going to be hard to explain."

"Well, if it should turn out he isn't our perp, you could always go ahead and have him build the bookcases. I think it would look really cool."

"I don't even want to think of that possibility. If that's the case we're screwed."

"Come on, Ty. No doom and gloom tonight. Come help me with the baggies."

We gathered everything together in a brown grocery sack.

"Now that we have it what do we do with it?" Ty asked. "Did you plan to walk into the police department with it?"

"They probably wouldn't listen to us. I think we need to go to Cliff and tell him the whole story of what we've been doing. We can say we did it because we wanted to take a load off his shoulders after his heart attack."

"You really think that will fly?"

"Maybe, maybe not. He might be mad as hell at us. But, after all, it's the Rinehart's lives that are at stake. They're more important than Cliff's feelings. And if he makes a fuss I intend to tell him just that."

"Since this evidence was gathered in a way that probably breaks every rule in the book, do you think the police will accept it?"

That thought really hadn't struck me until now. I'd been so excited at the idea of getting Tom's fingerprints I didn't think it through. I felt a little nauseous at the thought it could all be for naught. "If nothing else, it should point the finger at him. They can get his fingerprints in their own strictly-by-the-book way."

"Let's hope."

"So, first thing tomorrow we go to Cliff?" I asked.

"Yep. And be prepared for fireworks. Even though the Fourth is long over."

THIRTY-FIVE

IT WAS WITH trepidation that I called Greta the next morning and asked if Ty and I could come see Cliff.

"You haven't been here for a meal in a long time," she said. "Why don't you come for dinner?"

"It's urgent," I said. "We really need to see him this morning."

"Then why don't you come on when you're ready and have your talk with him. Then plan to stay for lunch."

"You don't have to go to all that trouble," I said thinking if Cliff got really mad at us it could be uncomfortable trying to get through a meal.

"I insist. You were so good to visit him in the hospital this is the least I can do."

I didn't want to keep arguing with her so I agreed. "We should get there between nine-thirty and ten."

When I called Ty he too was reluctant to stay for lunch, but I explained to him I didn't want to hurt her feelings.

We met in the lobby about twenty till ten and drove to the Holcomb's house. Greta, as always, met us at the door with a welcoming smile. "It was nice to see Ty the other day," she said, "but I've missed seeing you Auntie. Are you doing all right?"

"I'm great," I said thinking at least I am until Cliff explodes from the news we brought.

"Cliff's in his study," Greta said. "He'll be right out."

"Is he trying to work from home?" Ty asked.

"A little just to keep his hand in. He promised me he wouldn't overdo."

Yeah right, I thought.

She called up the stairs to tell him we were there. In a minute he came bouncing down them in obvious good shape. No wonder he was getting stir-crazy.

"Hey guys," he said cheerily. "I've got some news for you. Maybe we should go to my study to talk."

"You can use the living room," Greta said. "I'm going to be out in the kitchen fixing lunch." She was used to being excluded from private conversations. "But I'll bring you all some coffee before you get started if you like."

"I like," I said. Ty and I had missed our usual coffee in the café although I always have a cup for breakfast.

"Me too," Ty added.

"I'll have another cup too," Cliff chimed in.

We limited our conversation to small talk until the coffee was delivered and Greta had gone back in the kitchen to stay.

"You have some news?" Ty asked. I knew he was anxious to hear anything relating to Arthur Tisdale.

"The police got a search warrant based on what they saw on Roberto's laptop. I think they are about to pick up Billy for questioning. I'm feeling good about this. I think your friend may be off the hook in another day or two."

"Well, we heard he was being released from the hospital, so that will surely be good news for him. I hope everyone at Glendon Hills greets him with open arms." I was glad I'd decided to get involved even when my instincts were telling me not to. There's nothing worse than seeing an innocent person pay the price for someone else's crime.

"They should," Ty said. "After all the rumors they spread, they should feel ashamed of themselves."

"It's human nature," Cliff said. "So why are you two

so anxious to see me this morning? Don't tell me you've gotten yourselves into some other mischief."

This was the moment I'd been dreading. But there was nothing to do but spell it all out.

I wanted to begin in the most conciliatory manner possible. "We know how hard it's been for you not to be able to personally attend to your cases since your heart attack and surgery," I began. "We were sure your absence put a great burden on your staff. So when Lawrence and Deborah Rinehart asked if we could help them, we thought we could not only help them but you as well. The more we could find out, the less you would have facing you when you were able to go back to the office."

Cliff's features went from cheerful to stormy during those few sentences. "Do you not think I'm capable of providing them a good defense?" he asked frowning.

Ty jumped right in. "We know you are one of the best, Cliff. It was just that the Rineharts were going through a very bad patch. They didn't know what was going on, and I think they just wanted assurances that someone was able to get on it right then. We didn't really expect to find anything," I'm not sure where he got that idea but if it helped calm Cliff down that was okay, "but it happens we did. That's what we want to share with you now."

The surge of agitation was visible on Cliff's face. I prayed we weren't endangering his health by dropping this bomb on him. But I had determined we were going to do this for the Rineharts' sake, and I was sticking to that.

He sighed deeply a couple of times. Finally he said, "Okay. What have you got?"

"It's a long story," I said. "And I need to start at the beginning."

And so we launched into the tale, Ty and I alternating telling him every twist and turn. We told how we interviewed the employees as well as Jeremy's sister, how we even went to the TV station to talk to the staff.

"Did you hear about the fund-raiser he started called the X Factor?" I asked.

"You mean the TV show?"

"No, he was raising money for research on histiocytosis X which is a disease that can kill children. He claimed online that his niece suffered from it but apparently no niece exists. Evidently he was pocketing all the money he raised," Ty said.

Cliff put his head in his hands. "My god, the guy was an SOB."

"It turned out that had no bearing on the case, but I think it puts a spotlight on the kind of person he was," I went on with the story, "We then learned nobody knew where an employee of the ad agency had gone who'd been fired a couple of weeks before Jeremy was killed. We were able to track her down finally and she told me the story of how Jeremy died. She'd been asked to help dispose of the body, and when she refused, they threatened her."

"How did you manage to get that out of her?"

"Lawrence offered her money and she was in pretty desperate straits."

"So tell me how it happened."

I related Roz's story as close to word-for-word as I could remember. "The problem was she didn't know who they called to help move the body after she turned them down."

"Did you find the answer?" Cliff asked.

"We put our heads together and used the process of elimination to come up with the probable perp," Ty said. "We figured it was Candice Knowlton's estranged husband. It had to be someone who could move a body easily and leave it so far out in the woods."

By this point Cliff was on his feet circling the room like

a caged tiger. Was he that upset with us or was he like this normally when working on a case?

"That's all well and good," he said, "but it takes more than hunches to arrest someone."

"We have more than a hunch," I said. "We have his fingerprints. We think they'll probably match prints left on the Rineharts' car when he planted the blood in the trunk and on the tarp where he put the hairs."

"My god, woman, how did you get those?"

"We invited him over to give us an estimate on building a bookcase in my apartment," Ty answered in my place, trying to shield me from Cliff's anger. "Vi, who played my wife, had tea and cookies for him and made sure we got his prints not only on the glass but on the plate as well. We brought them over to give you."

Cliff studied the ceiling for a few minutes. I didn't know if he was looking for an answer from heaven or what.

"I don't know what to say to you two. Do you realize how much risk you are taking when you do things like this? I'd never forgive myself if anything happened to you."

"We're adults," I said trying to keep the anger out of my voice. I had scooted to the edge of the davenport in my fervor to get my point across. "I think we're capable of making that decision ourselves. We are always extremely careful not to put ourselves in harm's way."

"What about inviting that guy into Ty's apartment?"

"He had no idea we were doing anything other than interviewing him as a craftsman. And there are places all around the apartment where there are cords to pull in emergencies," I told him. I didn't say I was afraid I was too far away from them to help if anything went wrong. "We were perfectly safe."

"So where is this evidence? You realize that it's probably useless since it wasn't obtained properly."

"We thought of that," Ty said. "But we hoped you could see if the prints match the ones taken from their car. Wouldn't that be enough to prompt the police to get his prints in a way that would satisfy the rules and regulations?"

Cliff stopped his pacing. "Well, are you going to give it to me?" I noticed he didn't answer Ty's question. He probably wasn't sure himself.

Ty hopped up. "Sure. I left it in the car. I'll go get it."

When he was out of the door, Cliff stopped in front of me. His eyes had sparks in them now. "Vi, I hope you're not trying to make a fool of me."

I stood up to face him. "I love you to death, Cliff. I would never want to do that. But you must understand that the Rineharts were desperate, and as long as they thought I could help them I was willing to give it a try. That seemed more important to me than not bruising your ego."

His eyes opened wide in shock. I suppose no one had ever spoken like that to him before. Finally he said, "You're quite right, Vi. I was letting my ego get in the way. This whole enforced 'vacation' has me on the edge. I can't stand doing nothing all day. And the idea that you two were running around doing what I or my staff should have been doing was too much. I'm sorry."

"Don't apologize. Just help us see this through to the end. We can't do it without you."

Ty came back at that moment with the brown bag and handed it to Cliff. "There's a glass, a plate, and even a paper napkin that have his prints all over them. I guess you'll need ours for the process of elimination."

"Yes. After lunch let's all go down to the station. I'll turn this over and talk to the D.A. and you two can get fingerprinted. You'd better watch out, though. That means your prints will now be in the system."

"Oh lord, Ty, we'd better watch ourselves now," I said. We all laughed which broke the tension.

THIRTY-SIX

GRETA SERVED US a delicious lunch of gazpacho, shrimp salad sandwiches and cappuccino crunch ice cream for dessert.

"It's too hot to bake," she said. "I hope this is okay."

"It hits the spot," I told her.

Ty was equally enthused.

As soon as we were done, Cliff told her we all had business at the police station. "I don't know when I'll be home."

"Please don't overdo, honey," she said.

"Greta, please don't hover. I'll be careful,"

We were on our way to the door, Cliff and Ty ahead of us. I reached over and gave Greta a hug. "He's just frustrated from having to sit around," I whispered to her.

She nodded, but there were tears in her eyes.

"He'll be fine." Poor Greta. This enforced "hiatus" was as hard or harder on her than it was for him.

We drove downtown in Ty's car while Cliff took his own. He said he had no idea how long he might have to stay. We parked in the lot across the street and walked into the station with him. He took us to the area where they do fingerprinting and introduced us to the officer in charge.

"We'll need the prints off these fine people for elimination, Sergeant Baker. I'll leave them in your hands." He told him which case file they'd go in and then left to visit the D.A.

It felt strange to have my fingers held by an officer, placed on an ink pad one by one, and rolled onto the proper sheet. I could tell Ty was feeling a little weird about it too. I was relieved when we left the station. "You don't suppose Cliff is cooking up some kind of retaliation for messing with his case do you?" I joked on our way to the car.

"Don't know. But we're in the system now. We'd better behave ourselves."

We heard nothing from Cliff the rest of the day. At dinner I told Ty I prayed they'd follow up and bring closure to the case. "I'll not feel totally secure as long as Tom Knowlton is running around loose. What if he figures out what we were doing?"

"I don't see how he can," Ty reassured me.

The next day Cliff called me early in the morning. "I convinced them to take another look at the case. That's the good news. The bad news is it's going to take a while. Seeing as how it's Friday I don't know how much will happen over the weekend since the case isn't brand spanking new. So have patience."

"I'll try, Cliff." I was thinking *that should be your motto Cliff.*

Ty and I went to the exercise room and did our rounds of the equipment. We were at loose ends now since there wasn't much more we could do for either the Rineharts or Arthur Tisdale. It was out of our hands. Then we went to lunch where we were served pimento cheese sandwiches and a bowl of cherry Jell-o. We ate in silence as we were past the point of grousing about it.

I was back in my apartment after lunch when Cliff called me again.

"That was fast," I said. "I thought it was going to take a while."

"This isn't about the Rineharts. I called to tell you they've arrested Billy Bates for arson."

"Yay!" I yelled in his ear. "Oops, sorry. Hope I didn't deafen you."

"That's okay. The ringing should stop soon."

"That should be a good omen. If they took the evidence we gave you to arrest him, they should be willing to use the fingerprints we got to arrest Tom Knowlton."

"That remains to be seen, Vi."

"Oh, okay. Well, thanks for calling. That's great news."

I called Ty immediately and asked him to meet me in the lobby.

"What's up?" he asked when we got there.

"I've got great news and I want to celebrate."

"Is this about the Rineharts?"

"No. They've arrested Billy Bates for arson. Why don't we go see Arthur at the hospital and give him the good news? I doubt anyone's told him yet."

"Well guess what? I ran into our favorite gossip on the way down here, and she told me they're releasing Arthur from the hospital this afternoon. He should be here at any time."

"I wonder if he has transportation. Why don't you call and see if we can pick him up."

He pulled his cell phone off his belt and called him. It turned out he was going to call a cab so Ty told him we'd be over to bring him home.

When he hung up he said, "He told me to come at four," He looked at his watch. "It's almost three now so why don't we leave here in about forty minutes?"

"Okay, then let's go talk to Frank Kaufman. Administration probably hasn't heard the news about Billy's arrest. They need to know that Arthur is innocent."

When we told Frank a look of great relief spread over his features. "What good news that is," he said. "After the terrible incident with Ralph Duncan last March we didn't need any more residents implicated in serious offenses. It would really give Glendon Hills a black eye."

I was a lot more concerned for Arthur's well-being than I was for Glendon Hill's reputation.

"I think we ought to do something to show our appreciation for Arthur's attempt to keep the fire from becoming much worse," I said. "He probably saved lives by getting the bottles of rum out of there."

I could see the gleam in Frank's eye as an idea came to him. "What a great idea, Viola. Maybe we should have some kind of a ceremony where we honor him in front of all the residents. We could probably even get the newspaper to cover it."

Cynic that I am, I'm sure he had good P.R. for GH uppermost in mind.

"Why not wait and see how he feels about it? He might find it embarrassing," Ty said.

We left it at that and went to pick up Arthur.

His arms were still wrapped in light bandages, but otherwise he was looking healthy.

Once we were in my car which we drove because Ty's car only holds two, I said to Arthur, "I don't know if you've heard this yet, but the police have arrested Billy Bates for setting the fire in our kitchen."

"Who the heck is Billy Bates?"

"He was a busboy who got fired a couple of weeks before the fire. He was mad and decided to start a small blaze just to aggravate them. He never intended it to get out of hand the way it did."

"Oh my god. I was expecting to get arrested at any minute. When that didn't happen, I figured they'd do it as soon as I got back home. How did they find out it was Billy?"

"Oh, they did a lot of digging," Ty said. "Thank goodness they didn't just settle on the most obvious suspect which was you."

Ty was sitting in the front seat beside me, and I reached over and patted his leg. Good for him for not wanting any credit.

When we arrived at the front door, Frank Kaufman was there to greet Arthur. We left at that point and went into the café where we both had a cup of decaf due to the late hour.

Ty raised his cup in toast and I raised mine and tapped it.

"One down and one to go!" he said.

THIRTY-SEVEN

THE WEEKEND DRAGGED by making the two days seem closer to two weeks. Both Ty and I were at loose ends. He played bridge while I read and watched TV, something I rarely do during the day.

On Monday morning they announced the reopening of the dining room. That seemed to be the main topic of conversation throughout the building. At noon Ty and I were eating lunch when Cora Lee came by our table. Leaning over us to speak in a low voice, she said, "I see Arthur Tisdale is back. I'm surprised they haven't arrested him yet." Arthur must have skipped the weekend meals, probably because he heard how dreadful they were. This might have been the first time he appeared in public.

"You mean you hadn't heard they arrested Billy Bates, a former busboy, for starting the fire?" Ty asked in a tone that indicated he was shocked she wasn't aware of it. He loved rubbing it in that for once she was out of the loop.

Her look was crestfallen. "Oh, I didn't know." And with that she left.

After she was gone we did a high five.

The weather had cooled off a bit so we drove to one of the city parks and walked around admiring the gardens.

It wasn't until Monday night I heard from Cliff.

"They've issued warrants for the arrest of the two women and Tom Knowlton. They were able to get his fingerprints at his workplace, and you'll be delighted to hear they matched those on the car."

"I hope it's not too late for the women to plead self defense," I said.

"That will be between them and their lawyer. Tom will be charged with accessory after the fact. His sentence will probably depend on how the women are charged. At any rate they'll all get some jail time."

"That's good. Do me a favor Cliff? I'm a little nervous about Tom. He may have figured out how the police got on to him. I'd like to know when he's in custody."

"Of course, Vi. If you're that worried maybe I can arrange some police protection for you."

"I don't think that's necessary. They have pretty tight security around here."

I called Ty immediately and told him the news.

"Look, Vi," he said, "I don't like the idea of you being alone in your apartment as long as Tom Knowlton is out there. I'm coming over to stay with you."

"You don't need to do that. I'll be okay. Besides I don't have a guest room."

"I'll sleep on the sofa. We'll *really* give Cora Lee something to talk about."

I laughed. "It would almost be worth it just for that."

A half an hour later he was there with an overnight bag.

"Did anyone see you coming in my apartment with that bag?" I asked him.

"No, don't think so," he grinned.

"Oh, darn."

We spent the evening playing double solitaire. I know Ty must have found it exceedingly boring, but I enjoyed it.

The night went without incident. The next morning I told him it was a waste of time for him to stay with me.

"I don't think so. As long as he's on the loose, I intend to spend the night."

"Well, go play bridge today and enjoy yourself. It's

bound to be more challenging than solitaire. He's not going to attack me in broad daylight."

He grudgingly agreed. We went to lunch together and parted afterward. Ty went to bridge, and I went back to my apartment to do some paperwork. The one thing that made me feel safe was the fact Tom thought I was Ty's wife and lived in his apartment.

I was trying to balance my bank statement when there was a knock on the door. I wondered if the bridge game was over already though it seemed early. They often played till dinner time. I looked through the peephole but couldn't see anything so I cautiously opened the door, and as soon as it was slightly open a powerful force slammed against it sending me flying backward onto the floor. I fell on my well-padded backside but I was in shock. At my age I can't scramble to my feet once I'm down. It's a difficult process to get up again. Once I came to my senses I looked up to see Tom Knowlton towering over me, his face red with anger.

"You bitch. You tricked me, didn't you?" he snarled.

"How did you know where I lived?" It was a stupid question at such a dangerous time but I was exceedingly curious to know how he tracked me down.

"You gave your real name to Missy and Candy when you talked to them. It was easy enough to get your apartment number after that. I'm going to make you pay for this. And then I'll take care of that so-called husband of yours."

I started to scoot backwards on my fanny to get away from him but it was futile. He reached over, grabbed my right arm and hauled me to my feet. It felt like he was pulling my arm out of its socket. I could see his eyes casing the apartment to figure out what to do with me. The longer I could stall him with questions, the better the chance that Ty would return.

"Tom, I know you're furious at what we did. But you weren't the one who killed Jeremy. We know that."

"That isn't going to make a hell of a lot of difference to the cops. They're gonna throw me in a cell for a good long time."

"Well, tell me this. Why did you decide to plant the hair and blood at the Rinehart's house? What did they ever do to you?"

"If he hadn't hired that sleazebag, this whole thing wouldn't have happened. The blame all goes back to him. He should have known that dude was bad news."

He was losing interest in my questions. He scowled at me. "So, your apartment and this Ty guy's are identical," he said. It was a statement not a question.

"No, his has an extra bedroom."

I wondered what his point was. If only I could get to my bedroom or bathroom I could pull the emergency cord for help. But that seemed like a remote possibility.

"But you both have a balcony," he went on.

It was beginning to become clear to me what he was planning. An icy chill began coursing through my veins. Sweetie could survive a fall from it, but I was pretty sure I could not.

Sweetie had been asleep in the bedroom but she came running out at the sound of voices. Somehow she sensed I was in danger, and she lunged for his leg and grabbed his pant's leg in her teeth.

"Stupid cat," he roared, and he swatted her so hard she flew several feet before landing. She lay still for a minute but then got up again to stage another attack. I was afraid he would kill her if she kept it up.

"Go, Sweetie. Go away," I pleaded.

But she didn't heed and went for his leg again. He grabbed her by the scruff of the neck, let go of me, and strode to the bedroom where he threw her in and slammed the door.

That gave me just enough time to pick up a brass statuette that was on an end table, rush over behind him and whack him over the head with all my strength. He crumpled instantly to the floor in a heap.

I ran out the door, took the stairs down and ran to the multi-purpose room where the Bridge Dudes were playing.

With no apologies or excuses I grabbed Ty's arm and pulled him to his feet. "You've got to come now. Tom's here." The other men looked at me like I had totally lost it, and truly I felt as if I had.

We both ran back to the front desk where I told Patricia to call the police and our security as well. "Tell them both to come to my apartment. There's a dangerous man inside. We need security to see that he's restrained until the police come."

I started back down the hall but Ty caught me by the arm. "You can't go back there," he said. "You've got to wait till the cops get here."

"I knocked him unconscious. He should still be out."

"You don't know that. Let security take care of him. We'll wait here till they get backup."

I realized he was right. We didn't have to wait very long. In a few minutes two patrol cars came roaring up out front, lights flashing and sirens going. This was going to be real entertainment for the residents of Glendon Hills. I told them very briefly what had happened and led the way to my apartment. They had us stand back while they drew their guns and stood on either side of my door calling out, "Police. Come out with your hands up."

Brad, our security guard, cautiously opened the door with his hands raised. "I'm security," he said, "The intruder is restrained and lying unconscious over by the bedroom door. What did you hit him with, Ms. Weather-spoon?" he asked me. "He's out cold."

"It's that brass thing over there on the floor I was given when I retired. The party had an Oscar theme and that's the reason for the statuette. It's inscribed '*To our hard working Executive Director. Best wishes for a peaceful retirement.*'"

Everyone had a good chuckle over that.

The police called the EMTs to make sure Tom wasn't seriously injured before taking him out on a stretcher.

"We'll take him to the jail infirmary until he's awake," they said.

"Do you realize he's wanted in the murder of Jeremy Scofield?" I asked.

They hadn't so they called the lead investigator on the case, and he said he'd meet them at the jail.

After they had all left, Ty and I sprawled on facing chairs utterly exhausted. My heart hadn't stopped pounding since Tom first came in the door. I hoped I wasn't going to have a heart attack. But it was finally beginning to slow down.

Suddenly I jumped up. "Oh no. Sweetie's still in the bedroom where he threw her when she attacked him. That was what gave me a chance to grab the 'Oscar' and hit him over the head. Otherwise I'd be toast my now. I'm pretty sure he was going to throw me off the balcony."

"I feel terrible I left you alone. I never dreamed he'd have the balls to come in broad daylight. And how did he know where you lived?"

"He found out my real name from Missy or Candy. Then it was simple. And he probably thought he'd be less conspicuous during the day when so many people are coming in and out," I said as I leveraged myself slowly out of the chair realizing how much I ached. I opened the bedroom door and Sweetie came running out and stopped suddenly to look around. I think she was looking for Tom so she could attack him again.

I picked her up and held her as I petted her with a grateful heart. "Do you realize Sweetie that you started this whole crazy thing, and you ended it as well? I believe I owe you my life. I'm going to get you the finest cat food money will buy and a nice new toy to boot."

"How about I get her a lifetime supply of catnip," Ty added.

We did another high five and collapsed back into our chairs. I dropped off into a peaceful doze and dreamed of all the books we would buy for the library.

* * * * *

REQUEST YOUR FREE BOOKS!

2 FREE NOVELS
PLUS 2 FREE GIFTS!

WORLDWIDE LIBRARY®

Your Partner in Crime

YES! Please send me 2 FREE novels from the Worldwide Library® series and my 2 FREE gifts (gifts are worth about $10). After receiving them, if I don't wish to receive any more books, I can return the shipping statement marked "cancel." If I don't cancel, I will receive 4 brand-new novels every month and be billed just $5.49 per book in the U.S. or $6.24 per book in Canada. That's a savings of at least 31% off the cover price. It's quite a bargain! Shipping and handling is just 50¢ per book in the U.S. and 75¢ per book in Canada.* I understand that accepting the 2 free books and gifts places me under no obligation to buy anything. I can always return a shipment and cancel at any time. Even if I never buy another book, the two free books and gifts are mine to keep forever.

414/424 WDN F4WY

Name	(PLEASE PRINT)
Address	Apt. #
City	State/Prov. Zip/Postal Code

Signature (if under 18, a parent or guardian must sign)

Mail to the Harlequin® Reader Service:
IN U.S.A.: P.O. Box 1867, Buffalo, NY 14240-1867
IN CANADA: P.O. Box 609, Fort Erie, Ontario L2A 5X3

Want to try two free books from another line?
Call 1-800-873-8635 or visit www.ReaderService.com.

* Terms and prices subject to change without notice. Prices do not include applicable taxes. Sales tax applicable in N.Y. Canadian residents will be charged applicable taxes. Offer not valid in Quebec. This offer is limited to one order per household. Not valid for current subscribers to the Worldwide Library series. All orders subject to credit approval. Credit or debit balances in a customer's account(s) may be offset by any other outstanding balance owed by or to the customer. Please allow 4 to 6 weeks for delivery. Offer available while quantities last.

Your Privacy—The Harlequin® Reader Service is committed to protecting your privacy. Our Privacy Policy is available online at www.ReaderService.com or upon request from the Harlequin Reader Service.

We make a portion of our mailing list available to reputable third parties that offer products we believe may interest you. If you prefer that we not exchange your name with third parties, or if you wish to clarify or modify your communication preferences, please visit us at www.ReaderService.com/consumerchoice or write to us at Harlequin Reader Service Preference Service, P.O. Box 9062, Buffalo, NY 14269. Include your complete name and address.

WWL13R

Reader Service.com

Manage your account online!

- Review your order history
- Manage your payments
- Update your address

---

*We've designed
the Harlequin® Reader Service
website just for you.*

Enjoy all the features!

- Reader excerpts from any series
- Respond to mailings and
  special monthly offers
- Discover new series available to you
- Browse the Bonus Bucks catalog
- Share your feedback

Visit us at:
ReaderService.com